The Mystery of
The Old Violin

(Original title: THE INN OF THE TWIN ANCHORS,
from THE RIDDLE AT LIVE OAKS)

By AUGUSTA HUIELL SEAMAN

Illustrated by William Hutchinson

Published by Scholastic Book Services, a division of Scholastic
Magazines, Inc., 33 West 42nd Street, New York 36, N.Y.

 This TAB edition is published by arrangement with Doubleday & Co., Inc. Published 1960 by Scholastic Book Services.

Printing History

1st printing................March, 1960
2nd printing...............March, 1961

Printed in the U.S.A.

To

the sunny memory of

"Julie"

(Julia Mae Brower)

this book is lovingly

dedicated.

Other books by Augusta Huiell Seaman

*THE MYSTERY OF THE EMPTY ROOM

*THE RIDDLE OF THE LONELY HOUSE

*A TAB book

CONTENTS

Chapter I

VISITORS AT TWILIGHT

THE SUN sets before five in the late October afternoons, and darkness draws in very soon afterward.

Marcella Danby came over the dunes and down the road at a snail's pace and turned in at the white gateposts of the Inn. Just for an instant, she raised her eyes to the two great ship anchors, each topping one of the high square solid pillars at the entrance. They were ancient ship anchors, salvaged from some long-past wreck, and had been where they were as far back as anyone could remember. The quaint old inn took its name from them.

Marcella noticed that the low, level rays of the setting sun had stained their dull surfaces a deep red, against the dark green cedars behind them. The colors pleased her. Then her thoughts were suddenly shifted elsewhere. There was a shiny, luxurious-looking car standing in the yard of the Inn.

"Visitors!" thought Marcella excitedly. "I wonder if they've come to stay overnight or only to dinner?"

She rushed into the office to find out. But the office was empty. The hotel register was lying open on the long desk. That must mean an overnight guest. And her father must have taken the person—or persons—upstairs to see the rooms. They would be coming down soon, no doubt. She slipped off her jacket and cap and sat down near the stairs to await them.

During the quiet fall and winter months the arrival of infrequent guests at the Inn was the biggest excitement in Marcella Danby's life. For the rest, her days were a simple round of attending school in the nearest town—going back and forth by bus—playing in her free hours on the endless dunes that flanked the sea behind the Inn, and being a companion to her lonely father. He owned the Inn and ran it mainly for the benefit of the more frequent summer tourists. When the summer was over, days often passed without a single guest arriving, except for an occasional meal, as the Inn was well away from the more frequented highways. It was an odd life for a girl of eleven, but Marcella had known no other since babyhood, was entirely used to it, and even liked it.

She sat for quite a while more watching the stairs, and still no one came down. The whole place was very quiet. The only other occupants of the house were old Samantha the cook, and David, her husband, who was waiter and handy man about the place. They were now busy in the kitchen at the far end of the house.

At last the quiet began to seem rather strange. Marcella decided to wait no longer but to go upstairs herself and see what it was all about. The last glow had faded from the west and the house was almost in darkness. Why had no one turned on the lights?

She crept up the wide white stairway hesitantly, expecting every moment to hear her father emerging from some room on the rambling floor above. But still the quiet persisted. Then, with her foot on the topmost step, she peered down the upper hall and noticed that the light was streaming from the open door of one of the bedrooms. But, singularly enough, all was as silent as if there were not a soul in the house. Surely, she thought, if her father were there with some guest, there would be the sound of conversation and probably footsteps. This silence was so unusual that she determined to go down the hall and investigate. She was only halfway there when she was startled to hear shouts from the interior of the room:

"What's *a marine bivalve mollusk?* Hurry up!"

"Can't think!" cried another voice. "What's *dislike greatly?*"

"*Hate,* you goose!"

"No, it isn't. It's got six letters."

"I don't know then. Look in the *dic!*"

There was complete silence again after this. Marcella crept forward and peered in the open doorway. To her astonishment, she beheld two children of about her own age. One of them, a girl, was seated on the bed, cross-legged, busily writing something in a book. A boy who wore large, dark-rimmed spectacles was lying flat on his stomach on the floor similarly engaged with a book and pencil. Both of them seemed to erase madly anything they wrote almost as soon as they got it down. There was a fat little book that looked like a dictionary lying open on the bed beside the girl. There was no sign of Mr. Danby anywhere about. Suddenly the girl looked up and saw Marcella standing in the doorway. Whereupon she dropped her pencil and straightened up with a jerk, demanding:

"Who are you?"

The boy also looked up, but exhibited no surprise at beholding Marcella, and inquired plaintively:

"I say, can *you* think of a word for *marine bivalve mollusk?*"

"I—I'm afraid I can't!" quavered Marcella, too surprised for any connected thought. "I—I'm Marcella Danby. I live here. Do you—do you happen to know where my father is?"

"Oh, is he the man who was showing us the rooms?" inquired the girl, in not too friendly a voice.

"Yes, he's Mr. Danby, my father, and he owns this hotel. I wonder where he's gone," replied Marcella.

"Well, I can tell you that," offered the boy. "We came here a while ago with Dad and Mother. We're going to stay quite a while, I guess—if we like it and it agrees with Dad. He's gotten terribly overtired, and the doctor says he must have a long rest by the sea. They went out, after they took the rooms, and asked your father to show them the view of the sea from the dunes before it got dark. We wanted to go too, but

Mother said we'd get all wet and messy trying to wade —or something—and we'd better wait till morning. So they made us stay here. *Can't* you think yet of any word for *marine bivalve mollusk?*"

"If you'll tell me what you're doing," gasped Marcella, trying to take in all this information and answer his questions at the same time, "I'll try to think. Is it your spelling lesson?" This was greeted by a shout of laughter from the girl, but the boy explained very patiently:

"Oh, no! These are crossword puzzles. Didn't you ever do any?"

"No," said Marcella. "I've seen them sometimes in papers and magazines, but never in books like you have. Do you like them very much? It must seem like lessons."

"Not a bit. We're crazy about them," put in the girl rather loftily. "Mother and Dad got them for us first because it was something for us to do when we're traveling and keeps us quiet. We didn't like them so well at first, but now we love them. We each have a book with fifty puzzles. Where do you go to school?" Somewhat mystified by the crossword puzzle talk, Marcella was glad to shift to a subject she knew more about, and she answered eagerly:

"I go to Tuckerstown. There's no school nearer.

The bus passes here every day, and I take that. I'm in the graduating class."

"Well, we're going too," announced the girl. "We've got to keep on with school, even if we *are* in the country. But I suppose it'll be a lot different from our Philadelphia school."

"It's a very nice school!" declared Marcella stoutly, ruffled by the newcomer's superior air. "I have a lovely teacher."

"I'm sure it's a nice school," the boy added. "And I always wanted to go to a country school. They don't rush you round like the city ones. You have time to think about things. And I'll teach you to do crossword puzzles."

At this moment they heard Mr. Danby coming in downstairs with his guests. Marcella hastily excused herself and hurried away, lest she seemed to be intruding. But her mind was full of excitement at the thought of these unexpected and most unusual guests who were going to make such an extended stay, and she questioned her father about them when he was alone in the office a little later.

"They're a Mr. and Mrs. Burdick," he said, "and the children's names are Jack and Jill, I think—at least, that's what they were called. They'll probably be here several months if it agrees with Mr. Burdick. He's all tired out and wants a complete rest. She said they had to bring the children with them, as they couldn't very well afford to put them in a private boarding school, with all the other expenses they're under at present. And their only fear is that the children will be noisy and worry their father. But I told them that they'd be off most of the day at school and the rest of the time could play with you and not be around Mr. Burdick too much. So it's up to you, Marcella, to help keep them quiet and amused and contented, so that they'll all want to stay a long time. It's a lucky thing for us to have any staying guest at this off time of the year, and is going to help us out a lot. I was beginning to wonder how we would make ends meet this year and this will pull us through nicely. Remember, you are the hostess here, whenever children are concerned."

Marcella was very happy that night. She was often a little lonely during the winter months. There were no children who lived near enough to be companions for her and she welcomed this unusual chance of playmates her own age with real joy. From where she sat in the dining room at a small table with her father, she watched the Burdicks at their larger one and tried to imagine what sort of family they were. She liked Mrs. Burdick's sweet and patient manner and admired Mr. Burdick's thin, fine scholarly face. The children were restless and fidgety, probably from their long trip, and she could see that they worried their father quite a bit. So she decided to do her best to amuse them that evening and take them off their parents' hands.

"Do you play parchesi?" she asked them after dinner. "How would you like to sit by the open fire in the living room and have a game with me?"

"I never played it, but I'd like to learn," agreed Jack amiably, but Jill turned away with a little sniff and said she'd rather read a magazine. So Jack and Marcella set up the parchesi board by the fire, and Jill retreated to a far corner of the big living room and appeared to become absorbed in a book.

"She's kind of snifty at me because I said I'd teach you crossword puzzles," confided Jack in an undertone. "But you mustn't mind her. She'll snap out of it after a while!" And, sure enough, it wasn't long before Jill threw down the book, got up, and began rambling round the big room, staring at the collection of curios and antiques which helped to furnish it. A large spinning wheel in a corner drew her first, then the model of a full-rigged clipper ship over the mantel, and last she halted before a quaint, diamond-paned corner cupboard filled with curious, oddly shaped bottles of every description.

"What are all these?" she demanded at length, of no one in particular. There was no one in the room to answer her except Marcella, for Mr. and Mrs. Burdick had retired to their room, and Mr. Danby was busy in his office.

"Why, that's our bottle collection," Marcella enlightened her. "Every once in a while you find very strange, interesting things on the beach, especially after a big storm. Daddy and I like to go along and pick them up. We like the bottles best because they seem most interesting. We only save those that are very odd or different. See—I'll show you some of them!"

She left the parchesi board, and they all went over to the cupboard. Marcella indicated to them the most interesting of the collection, showing them some that were quite old and different from anything manufactured nowadays. But it was Jack who exclaimed excitedly:

"Say—that's great! I love to collect things. You ought to see my stamps. I'm going to begin to hunt old bottles tomorrow. Maybe I can get a worthwhile set before we go away!" But Jill was still unimpressed. It was evident that she at least did not have the collecting mania. Suddenly Marcella had an inspiration.

"If you're interested in things like that," she exclaimed to Jack, "I'll take you some day soon to see the museum that a man has down along the dunes. He's an awfully queer person. They call him the 'Hermit!' And he has a cabin just filled with all the queer things he's found on the beach along here for years and years. Ship figureheads and charts and things from old, wrecked vessels. You never saw such a strange lot of things! He says he's going to present them to the State Historical Museum when he dies. He's awfully nice and kind, too—but very queer. They say there's some mystery about him."

And now, at last, Jill exhibited signs of interest. It was plain that mysteries were the subjects that most appealed to *her!*

"What *is* the mystery about him?" she demanded in a tense whisper. "Can't you tell us more about it?" But at that moment Mrs. Burdick came into the room to gather her children off to bed. Both Jack and Jill put forth frantic pleas to be allowed to stay up a while longer, but Marcella, mindful of her father's warning, intervened:

"I'll tell you more about it tomorrow. It's Saturday, and we won't have to go to school." And with this promise they had to be content for the night.

Chapter II

A MORNING ON THE DUNES

THE NEXT MORNING, very soon after breakfast, the three children sallied out to the beach and began scrambling round among the dunes, searching for treasure trove in the way of odd or interesting bottles. They hadn't gone far when they saw that they were being followed by a an enormous maltese-and-white cat, who was stepping pompously along after them, waving a long and plumy tail.

"That's my cat—Boots," Marcella informed the new friends. "He often follows me like this if he's around when I go out. He's almost like a dog that way."

"I see why you call him 'Boots,'" remarked Jack, who was very observant. "His hind legs are white part of the way up, just like a pair of boots. Isn't that it?"

"You're right!" laughed Marcella. "I didn't think you'd guess it. He's a loving old goose when he's around, but he's a terrible tramp and spends days away in the woods sometimes. He just got back this morning, I guess, for he wasn't about all day yesterday." Boots rubbed against her legs in a friendly gesture and then proceeded to trot along after them when they once more got under way.

It was a marvelous October morning, golden with sunshine, the sea of sapphire blue breaking on the sand in crisp white-maned breakers.

"Gee, I love this!" cried Jack, inflating his lungs deeply with the salt, invigorating air. "I could stay out here all day. Couldn't you, Jill?"

"I like it too," agreed Jill, "but I'm crazy to see this hermit that Marcella told us about last night. Let's go right now, can't we? Where is his place, anyway? And what's the mystery about him?"

"It's way down the beach," replied Marcella, "about a mile. I'll take you there, if you like, but we'd better walk along the edge of the surf, because the sand's harder there. It isn't easy to walk in sand if you're not used to it. You get awfully tired. And I'll tell you about him as we go along."

"I'm tired right now!" groaned Jack. "I've been climbing up and down those dunes more than you two have. It's good hard work. Let's go sort of slowly and look for old bottles and things as we go along."

So they rambled down to where the waves broke on the sand, and strolled leisurely southward, keeping an off eye on all the flotsam and jetsam of many past storms as they went along. Once Jack pounced on a tall, slender old yellow jug with a tiny little handle up near the spout.

"Here's the first of my collection!" he shouted. "Isn't it a queer one?"

Marcella hated to tell him that its like was all too common almost anywhere along the beach. She only congratulated him and advised him to leave it where it was and mark the spot so that they could pick it up on the way back, as he would soon be tired carrying it all the way. And while they rambled along, dodging the waves that threatened to curl round them, she told them what she knew about "the Hermit of the beach," as he was called.

"Daddy told me his name is really Herbert Seymour, though everyone around here calls him 'Hermit Seymour.' That's because he lives all by himself, sort of like a hermit, you know."

"They call hermits 'eremites' in the crossword puzzle books!" murmured Jill somewhat irrelevantly. But Jack exclaimed impatiently:

"Oh, can't you forget puzzles when you have a mystery to talk about! They call 'em 'recluses' too, but what's that got to do with it? Go on with your yarn, Marcella!"

"All right!" agreed Marcella, somewhat bewildered by these occasional wordy sparring matches between the brother and sister. "Well, he's an old man—at least, he seems very old, for his hair is snow-white and very curly. But he's got nice twinkling blue eyes, and his face doesn't seem old if you don't look at his hair. And he's awfully strong and can walk miles and miles and lift heavy things—and all that. He built the little shack he lives in and the part he calls the 'museum' all by himself, out of timbers that came from the sea. There's loads and loads of lumber cast up on this beach after some of the big northeast storms. And I told you last night about how he's found or collected all the queer sort of bygone things that belong to the sea—old ship figureheads and anchors and compasses and bells. He once wanted Daddy to sell him the two old anchors on our gateposts to put in his collection, but Daddy said he couldn't do that because they'd always been there as long as anyone could remember, and the Inn takes its name from them."

"But what's the *mystery* about him?" interrupted Jill. "That's what *I'm* interested in!"

"I was just getting to that," explained Marcella. "The mystery is that, though he's lived here quite a long time all by himself, no one knows anything really about him. They don't know where he came from or why he lives here all by himself like that, or even if Herbert Seymour is his real name. He never tells anybody anything about himself. But one thing Daddy and I found out about him that I don't think anyone else knows. He's very musical and plays beautifully on the violin. We were walking down the beach late one night in the moonlight, and when we got near his shack we heard the most beautiful music played on a violin. But he must have heard the crunching of our footsteps in the sand, for right away it stopped and didn't go on."

"What kind of thing was he playing?" demanded

Jack, who was musical himself and had been taking violin lessons when he was at home.

"Daddy said he thought it was something from Chopin," replied Marcella, "but he couldn't be sure, because we heard so little and it left off so suddenly. It's queer, isn't it, that he won't let anyone know he plays so beautifully? I wonder why."

"But what does he do for a living?" demanded the practical Jill. "He must have to have some money for food and things, even if he does live in a lonely spot like this. Does he work at anything?"

"That's another queer thing," went on Marcella. "He doesn't work at anything for money, that we're certain of. And yet he always seems to have plenty to eat and for clothes and all he needs. He even *buys* some of those queer things for his museum from places along the coast here sometimes. If he hears of anyone who has some really old and interesting thing like a map or chart or figurehead or something, he'll go and offer them quite a good deal of money to buy the things. But no one knows where he gets that money."

"Maybe he's a pirate and has stolen it!" supplied Jill, with the vivid memory of *Treasure Island* and other pirate lore in her mind. Marcella laughed.

"No, you'd never think that if you saw him," she said. "He doesn't look or act the least bit like a pirate.

Daddy says he's one of the most perfect gentlemen he ever talked to, and awfully interesting besides. He has a lot of books in his shack, and sometimes he lends them to Dad. No, it isn't that! You'll have to guess again, Jill. But, look!—there's his shack, right along there between those two high dunes. He built it where it would be sheltered from the high northeast and northwest winds." They all gazed down the beach toward the odd-looking shack sheathed with tar paper and a long tin pipe that plainly served as a chimney, sticking up in one corner. It seemed to crouch down between the dunes as if begging shelter of their protecting bulk.

"What a queer looking dump!" sniffed Jill. "Is it as funny inside as it is outside?"

"*I* think it's great!" cried Jack. "I'd love to live in a place like that—all the year round."

"It's really quite nice inside," explained Marcella. "He has a lovely old Franklin stove—the kind, you know, that is really like an open fireplace—and he burns driftwood from the beach. He's made all of the furniture himself, and it's awfully nice. And with his books all around the room on shelves and one or two pictures, the place looks very cosy inside. I'm sure you'll think so too."

They made their way closer to the shack in the

dunes, and Marcella promised that if the Hermit were at home she would ask if they could come in and look at his museum, which was in a connecting building off to the back.

"I think he's home," she said, "because the front door is standing open. He always locks it when he goes down the beach or off anywhere. He must be inside or somewhere quite near."

In another moment they were standing before the door and peering curiously inside, while Marcella rapped loudly on the panel. But there was no answer, nor did anyone appear around the back of the house. Marcella ran lightly up the nearest dune, which was quite high, and scanned the horizon. Then she turned and came down.

"There's something awfully queer about this!" she whispered. "He doesn't answer, and he isn't anywhere about. He never left the place alone and open like this before. I wonder what has happened to him?"

Chapter III

A SEARCH BY THE SEA

"WELL—what are we going to do about it?" demanded Jill, as all three remained standing outside the shack undecidedly, peering in with curious glances at the really delightful cosiness of the inside view.

"I—I don't quite know," said Marcella uncertainly. "Somehow, I'd hate to go away and leave the place open like this, because someone might come along and walk in here and take something they oughtn't. And then, too, if we wait around a bit, he might come back from wherever he is."

"Maybe he's in the museum part," suggested Jack, "and hasn't heard us. Suppose we go around to the side and look in the window. It *has* a window, I see, over on that side toward the Bay." Marcella nodded, and they all scuttled around to the side. Standing on tiptoe, they peeped in at the uncurtained window. Through the lower pane they could observe the interior, crowded, as Marcella had told them, with marine curiosities of every description. But there was no hermit or any other living creature to be seen therein.

"No," declared Marcella, shaking her head, "he must be out somewhere. But if that's so, he must be quite far away, for I didn't see a sign of him from that high dune. I do wonder what can have happened!"

"Let's go back and tell your father," suggested Jack. "Maybe *he* can think what to do."

"But that would take quite a while," objected Marcella, "and I don't like to leave the place open, with no one around, and we haven't any key to lock it. And if he'd had an accident or was hurt somehow, it wouldn't be a good thing to leave him alone so long. Besides, I just remember that Daddy had to drive to town today to do a lot of marketing and will be gone all morning."

"I'll tell you what!" cried Jill, suddenly fired to unusual action by the mystery and difficulties of the case. "Let's get up a search party and see what's become of him. We'll all go different ways and come back to the shack here and report what we've found. And if any of us should suddenly find him, we'll yell as loud as we can and get the rest of us to the spot." She was all enthusiasm, having thought up the plan, no doubt, from some mystery tale she had been reading. But Marcella and Jack were somewhat dubious of its success.

"It's kind of dangerous," said Marcella, "for you two to be scrambling around here alone. There are some nasty marshy spots that you might get caught in and sink before anyone got to you. I know them because I've explored all around here with Dad. And you might get lost, too. It's awfully confusing when you get off in those bushes and woods near the Bay, if you don't know your way about."

"Well, then, let's all go together," cried Jill, not to be cheated of her search party. "Then you can tell us where *not* to go!"

"And let's close the door of the cabin, at least," added Jack, "for then a stranger coming along would probably think it locked."

The scheme appealed to Marcella as very sensible, so she pulled shut the door of the shack, and they set off across the dunes toward the Bay, as there had been no sign of the Hermit on the ocean side. It was Jill, at length, who proved the best detective of them all.

"Look here!" she suddenly shouted, bending down to examine something in the sand. They were following a little sandy path toward the Bay, on each side of which grew tall, sturdy sea grass. They had been walking single file, and Jill had been in the lead. At her shout, the others sprang to her side and looked along the path where she pointed.

"What is it?" asked Jack, bewildered. "I don't see anything to get excited about."

"Oh, I know what she means," said Marcella, "and I ought to be ashamed of myself for not having thought of it before. *Footprints!*—and they're most likely the Hermit's, so of course he went along this way."

"They're a man's, anyhow!" cried Jack, now all excitement. "Let's get going! If we follow these we'll surely come to something. Good for you, Jill!"

Filled with fresh enthusiasm, they hurried on along the sandy track, following closely, as they went, the heavy footprints of a man's rubber-soled and heeled shoe, the design of which was very distinct. There had been a light rain the night before, and it was evident that no other person had passed that way, nor had the one whose footprints they were following returned that way, for there was no sign of them in the reverse direction. On they hurried, through bayberry bushes and cat briar and occasional high cedar clumps, twisting with the crooked little path. And always the beckoning footprints led them on.

Suddenly they were all startled to have the cat, Boots, who none of them realized had been trotting along in their rear, suddenly go leaping lightly past all of them and disappear, flying around a bend where the path curved about some holly and cedar trees. But when they rounded that bend themselves, there was no Boots in sight anywhere.

"That's funny!" said Marcella. "He usually stays around with me when we're out walking. But I suppose he smelled a field mouse or something and is off after it." They went on tracing down the footprints and thought no more about the cat.

Suddenly Marcella, who was now ahead, stopped short, beckoned them to look, and demanded, "What do you think of *that?*"

Instead of the single line of footprints following one

another in regular strides, the sand in the path had been scuffled and tossed about, there were stray footprints here and there at either side, but there they stopped. And as far along the path as they could see there was no further trace of the tracks they had so long been following.

"Looks as if something had happened here," announced Jack. "But you can't tell what it was. If there were any other kind of footprints, I'd say there'd been a fight. But there aren't, and the funniest thing is, where did he go after that? He didn't go back and he didn't go on. Where——"

"Why, he went off to the side, you goose!" declared Jill scornfully. She had been doing some thinking on her own hook. "Look here!—this queer mossy-looking stuff here at the side of the path doesn't show any footprints. I just tried it."

"Yes, that's beach heather," said Marcella, "and when it grows close like that, it doesn't show footprints except when you walk over the same place a number of times. But which way did he go—right or left? There's a deep, marshy meadow on that left side, right beyond those bushes, and he'd just get stuck if he went through there. And over this side the cat briar is so thick you couldn't get through it without having your clothes torn right off your back. I don't think——"

"Oh, look!—*look!*" cried Jill, pointing suddenly to the bushes on the left side, beyond which Marcella had said was the marsh. "What's the matter with your cat? Do you see him, just his tail and hind legs sticking out of the bushes? And his tail is swishing back and forth as if he was terribly excited about something. Let's go see what he's found."

"It's probably only a bird or something like that," commented Marcella. Nevertheless they turned in Boots' direction, tiptoeing softly so as not to disturb him, and presently drew up directly behind him, where he was crouched, his head and shoulders well in the bushes that thinly screened the marsh beyond. He was so absorbed that he paid not the slightest attention to them. It was Marcella who parted the bushes above him, poked her head through, and took one long look about. In another instant she had pulled back her head with a little smothered cry of astonishment and fear.

"Oh, *look*—look in there!" she shuddered, pointing to the gap she had made by parting the bushes.

Chapter IV

WHAT THEY FOUND

JACK AND JILL needed no second invitation, but pushed by her and poked their heads through the gap. And then they too drew back with every sign of surprise and dismay.

"Who—who is it?" gasped Jill. "And what is the matter with him?"

"It's the Hermit—of course!" stammered Marcella. "And I think he's—hurt—or something! He's lying there —right in the marsh—I couldn't see his face—but his hands were grabbing the bushes—as if he was trying to keep himself from sinking. Boots must have known he was there. Mr. Seymour is very fond of Boots and always pets him when we come down here. Oh, *what* shall we do?" They all poked their heads through the gap again, and the cat padded over to sniff at the prostrate figure on the edge of the marsh.

"There's only one thing to do," declared Jack, "and that's to hurry right over and see what's the matter and then get some help. Why do we stand here talking about it?" They promptly broke through the bushes and ran to the side of the silent figure by the marsh. And as they got closer a new shock awaited them, for they saw at once that the Hermit was not lying on the marshy meadow, as they had first thought, but was sunk almost to his waist in mud and ooze, which explained his desperate grip on the sturdy groundsel bush that grew on the edge of the firm soil. There was every sign that he had struggled long and hopelessly to drag himself out. At the present moment he seemed to have lost consciousness, though his grip on the bush still held. Marcella bent down and cautiously placed her hand on his forehead. If he felt it, he made no response, and she called to him: "Mr. Seymour—Mr. Seymour, what is the matter? Let us help you out of here!" And at last, at the sound of her voice, the Hermit's eyes opened, and he shivered and looked up, dazed, scarcely recognizing who his rescuer might be.

"I—I have broken my ankle—I think. I—fell—stumbled in here afterward—I couldn't pull myself out—my ankle is so bad. I kept sinking—I called and shouted—till I lost my voice. This bush—all that kept me up. Then I—I gave up hope." He closed his eyes once more from sheer exhaustion. It was Jack, then, who constituted himself master of ceremonies and took charge of the occasion.

"Well, sir," he announced reassuringly, "don't you worry. We're here and going to pull you out. And we'll try to do it without hurting you." Again the Hermit opened his eyes and smiled in a feeble but grateful attempt to thank them.

"That is good of you," he gasped. "I can't hold out much longer or I'd tell you to go back home for help. But perhaps this is better. Go back to my house—one of you—and find a rope—just outside near the back. Bring it—quickly. I'll tell you what to do next."

"I know where it is!" cried Marcella, and raced back along the sandy path to fetch it. She was gone for what seemed hours to the waiting trio, but was really only five minutes. Then the Hermit directed them to make a noose of the rope, slip it over his shoulders and under his arms, and fasten it securely to the nearest stout bush. When this was done he tried to pull himself out by grasping the rope, and the three children helped as best they could by lifting him by the arms and prying his legs out of the ooze. Once he cried out in agony when Jack wrenched too firmly on the injured leg. It seemed an interminable and almost hopeless struggle, but at last the hungry oozy slime relinquished its prey and the poor Hermit lay gasping and in pain, but free at last, on the firm ground beyond the marsh. After that came the problem of getting him back to his shack. Plainly he could not walk, nor could the three children carry him. It was the resourceful Jack who once more solved the riddle.

"If you'll let us get a blanket from your bed," he suggested, "I think we could carry you in it, or pull you along on it so that it wouldn't hurt you much." The Hermit agreed, and Marcella and Jill rushed back to the shack and found a large double blanket on his couch, in the one room the shack contained. Getting him back on it was a painful process, despite the best they could do, but at last he was indoors and lying on his couch, while he directed Marcella to put cold wet cloths about his swollen ankle. All this time he had offered no explanation of why he had come to meet with such an odd and very nearly tragic accident, and the children politely refrained from questioning him. When he had been made as comfortable as they could make him, they stood about hesitantly, uncertain what to do next, till Marcella suggested:

"I think we'd better go back now and tell my father about your accident. He can get a doctor to help with your ankle and see what's best to do for you." To their utmost surprise, the Hermit lifted himself on his elbow and quietly but definitely refused this offer.

"Thank you, Marcella," he said weakly, "and you others whom I haven't met before, for all you've done for me. I'm sure you saved my life, for I couldn't have held out much longer. And my voice was so hoarse I couldn't call any more. But I don't think I need any doctor. I'm certain now my ankle isn't broken—only badly strained or sprained. I know how to treat that myself, for I'm a bit of a doctor in an amateur way, and I can do all that's necessary for it myself."

"But should you step on it?" cried Marcella.

The Hermit smiled at her concern.

"Oh, I'm prepared for everything," he reassured her,

"as I'll soon show you. Once I found a very good pair of crutches on the beach, only one of which was split and broken toward the bottom. I mended it, and they're both standing in the museum now. Will you get them for me, Marcella? With those, I'll be quite independent, for I can keep off my damaged ankle and still get around." Marcella did as he requested and placed a pair of very substantial-looking crutches by his side.

"Now I'm all set," he declared, "and when I feel a little rested, I'll bandage my ankle tightly and hop around on my crutches and get myself some lunch."

"Couldn't we get it for you?" suggested Marcella. But he refused this offer also, saying he did not feel like eating just then and would prefer to wait till later.

"Then, I guess we'd better go," said Marcella, "but I'll tell Daddy when he comes home about your accident, and he'll come down and see if he can get you anything you need. Good-bye!" But for some unknown reason her last suggestion seemed to upset the Hermit most unexpectedly, for he struggled to his elbow again and cried:

"Wait—wait! There is something, please, that I must beg of you not to do. It is a strange thing to ask, I know, but do not tell your father or anyone how you found me today, if you will be so kind. I cannot explain why I ask this, but I do beg that you will all do as I wish in this matter. It is most important—to me. Tell him I have sprained my ankle, if you will, and that I will be most grateful if he can visit me and obtain a few supplies for me while I am so crippled. But say nothing about—the rest. Will you promise?"

He was so earnest—so desperately earnest about it that they all murmured a promise, and he dropped back, relieved, on his couch. "And believe me," he added, "I shall never forget, as long as I live, what you have done for me this day." Solemnly and deeply impressed, they all murmured good-bye and filed out of the little shack, where Boots was waiting for them, curled up in a sunny, sheltered corner near the door. No one spoke a single word till they were out on the beach and well beyond hearing distance of the hut.

Then their tongues were unloosed and they began demanding of one another what it all meant, anyhow. It was to Marcella that Jack and Jill turned for an explanation, thinking she knew more about this curious person than they did. But Marcella was as much in the dark as themselves.

"It's no use to ask *me!*" she declared as they started to walk toward the Inn. "I can't imagine why he didn't want us to tell anyone about how and where we found him. Any more than I can think why he went out there and hurt his ankle and got caught in the marsh. And it makes me feel very queer not to be able to tell Daddy about it, but we just mustn't, since we promised. I don't suppose it's any of our business, anyway."

"There's something awfully queer about it—the whole thing," mused Jack. "But I like him, though. I think he's great! We must have hurt him terribly getting him out of there and dragging him home, but he never even groaned except once, when I didn't realize I was pulling on his foot so hard. He's fine-looking, too, with all that curly white hair and his nice kind eyes. I like him!"

"I liked his house, too," conceded Jill. "I couldn't do so much there as you and Marcella did, so I had time to look about a bit. It's so cosy and comfortable. And did he make all that nice furniture?"

"Yes," said Marcella, "he made every bit of it. He has a lot of fine tools in a shed outside and he can make lovely things. He made me the nicest little bench once. I have it in my room. But did you notice the beautiful cabinet on the wall, the one with the glass door? It has a violin hanging inside it. He made that cabinet too. It took him months and months to get it properly polished and finished—he was so careful about it. He made it to keep that violin in. It is such a beautiful old violin—he said it was a very rare and expensive one—that he wanted a suitable case to keep it in. It must be one that kept out the damp, yet would show the instrument, too, so he made the door of glass. He always keeps it locked. Did you notice it?"

"I didn't," said Jack, "for I was too busy helping you."

"Well, I did," declared Jill. "But I'm going to tell you something that'll surprise you. I saw that case all right, but the glass door was standing open—and there wasn't any violin inside it at all—or anything else. I thought it was rather queer—an empty cabinet like that with the door standing open. But I didn't like to say anything about it."

At this unexpected and surprising bit of information, Marcella stopped short and gaped at them both with the most startled expression in her eyes.

"You saw the case—and the violin wasn't in it—and the door was open?" she gasped. "I never even noticed—I was so busy trying to help with his poor ankle. But where can it be then? It wasn't lying anywhere around when we went in and out to get things. It wasn't in the museum, or I would have seen it. *Where* can it be?"

"No use asking *me!*" answered Jill. "But here's something that's puzzling me even more. Does *he* know it isn't there?"

"Good-*night!*" exclaimed Jack suddenly. "Maybe *that's* what he's all upset about!"

Chapter V

SEVERAL THINGS HAPPEN

IN THE WEEK that followed a number of things happened, not all of them connected with the affair of the Hermit. To begin with, on Monday morning, Jack and Jill, accompanied by their mother, set out in the bus with Marcella and were duly installed in the school in the next town. They were placed in Marcella's class, and before many days had passed were as enthusiastic as Marcella herself about the teacher and their lessons and began to think that going to school in the country was quite an absorbing affair. In the afternoons the three romped and explored on the beach, and in the evenings studied together quietly in the big living room of the Inn.

But in all these new interests they had not forgotten their curious and exciting adventure with the Hermit. On the contrary, it was constantly in their minds. Marcella had told her father, on their return that first amazing Saturday, that they had walked down to the Hermit's and found he had met with an accident that had sprained his ankle badly, and that they had left him lying rather helpless on his couch and asking that Mr. Danby would be so kind as to come down and see him. Mr. Danby had gone there, alone, that very afternoon.

On his return Marcella had asked him how he had found things, and he had replied with a rather puzzled expression:

"I found him hobbling around on that pair of crutches he says he once picked up on the beach after a storm. His ankle was bandaged with adhesive tape in what seemed a pretty expert way, and I guess that's going to be all right in time. He says he was hurrying through the bushes early Saturday morning and caught it unexpectedly in a trailing vine which threw him and twisted his ankle so badly that he could hardly get home. He says it was lucky you children came along this morning, as you were able to help him quite a bit and bring the message to me." Here Marcella swallowed hard and tried not to look as if she knew anything more about the affair than that.

"But what puzzled me," went on Mr. Danby, "was that he seemed terribly upset and worried and depressed about something or other that he didn't care to talk about. And when I asked him if he wouldn't like me to send David down to spend the night with him and help him, in case his ankle should grow any worse, he cried out, almost with horror:

" 'Oh, no, no, *no!* I do not need anyone. I am quite capable of taking care of myself.' All he'd consent to my doing was to buy him some supplies, which I did this afternoon, and promise him that you children would bring them down tomorrow. That seemed to please him. But I can't help but feel that something's radically wrong with him besides just having given his ankle a twist."

"Did he say anything about his violin?" queried

Marcella, unable to refrain from questioning on this point, which was something the Hermit had not forbidden them to speak about. Mr. Danby threw her a look of startled wonder.

"His violin? —Do you mean the Strad he always keeps in the case on the wall? Of course not. Why should he?"

"Because," said Marcella gravely, "it wasn't in the case today when we were there. The case door was standing open—and the violin was gone!"

"Whee-ee!" whistled Mr. Danby in some astonishment. "You don't say so! But, pshaw!—that mightn't mean anything. He might have just taken it out and put it down somewhere——"

"Oh, but it wasn't put down anywhere!" interrupted Marcella eagerly. "I know, because I was all over the place—even out in the museum to get his crutches for him. And it wasn't *anywhere!*"

"You don't *say!*" exclaimed Mr. Danby, impressed at last. "Well, maybe that's why he acted so strangely. Perhaps someone has gotten in and stolen it. It was an almost priceless instrument, he once told me, and it would be enough to upset anyone to lose it. But why didn't he speak about it, I wonder?"

"I don't know, Daddy. Only I think he doesn't want to talk about it, so I suppose we can't ask him."

"That's evident," said Mr. Danby. And there, for the time being, the matter ended.

The next morning the children carried down to the Hermit a parcel of groceries and supplies for him that Mr. Danby had obtained, and found him lying on his couch reading. He rose to greet them, however, and hobbled about quite expertly on his crutches, putting the things away. At Marcella's request, he allowed her to take the two newcomers into the museum and show them his treasures there, but did not try to come in himself or talk about them. They noticed that the violin case still hung on his living-room wall, but it was closed now—and empty. Marcella tried to screw up her courage to ask him what had become of the violin, but somehow did not dare to attempt it, for, contrary to his usual cheeriness, he seemed very quiet and disinclined to talk much. Presently they left him, promising to return in a day or so to see how he was getting on. He did not urge them to stay and seemed glad to be left alone, which, as Marcella assured the others later, was very unlike the way he usually acted. It was plain that something was sorely bothering him!

The children did not see him again till the following Wednesday though Mr. Danby or David had walked down every day, carrying food and supplies, and had kept watch to see that he was not in need of anything. But the weather had turned cold and rainy, and neither Marcella nor the other two children had been allowed to go out for any length of time on the beach. Wednesday afternoon, however, it had stopped raining and was warm and a trifle misty. After school the three children were permitted to range the beach once more, and Marcella was asked by her father to walk down to the Hermit's shack and leave some of Samantha's biscuits and a pie that she had cooked especially for him.

"There's one thing I'd like to know about the Hermit," declared Jill as they tramped along at the edge of the surf.

"There's a whole lot we'd all like to know!" grinned her brother. "But go on. Don't let us interrupt you!"

"Oh, hush!" cried Jill. "And let me finish what I'm saying. I keep wondering and wondering whether his going out that time and leaving his house all open and getting his foot hurt and getting caught in the marsh had anything to do with his violin being gone."

"But, of *course*—you silly! It had *everything* to do with it!" declared Jack scornfully. "Somebody got in during the night and stole his violin, and he woke up and found the case open and the thing gone. Then he hustled out to look for it, or perhaps to chase whoever took it, and he never even stopped to close his door.

And then, while he was running after them, he stumbled and caught his foot and wrenched his ankle. But even then he didn't stop, only he was so excited that he didn't look which way he was going till he got into the marsh and found himself sinking. I've thought it all out, and it's perfectly plain." Jill was quite impressed with her brother's reasoning and murmured:

"Yes, I suppose that's it." But Marcella ventured:

"I've thought of that too, only somehow it doesn't explain everything. If it had been just like that, I can't see any reason why he wouldn't have just said so—told us all about it. Why should he act as if he didn't want anyone to know what had happened—and why didn't he say a single word about the violin?"

"That's so," admitted Jack somewhat ruefully. "I never thought of it."

"And then there's another thing," went on Marcella. "You remember it had rained quite hard the night before—hard enough to flatten out all the footprints around his shack except what had been made after it stopped. Well, don't you remember that his footprints were the only ones we found—anywhere around there? That rain stopped before midnight. I heard Daddy say so next morning, because he'd been awake when it cleared. The Hermit told Daddy once that he *never* goes to sleep before midnight, but sits up and reads till very late. Then can you explain why there weren't some other footprints about except his, if someone had run off with the violin when he was asleep? For I'm certain they couldn't have got in and taken it while he was there in the room—awake and reading. Could they?"

The other two had to admit, reluctantly, that it didn't seem probable, and abandoned Jack's nicely constructed theory.

"But what *did* happen, then?" demanded Jill impatiently. And there Marcella had to admit that she was just as much in the dark as themselves.

"But there's always been something mysterious about that violin," she added. "He has shown it to us and told us that it was a very rare and wonderful instrument, made by someone called Stradivarius, centuries ago, and that they don't make them like that any more, and there are only a very few like it in all the world. But once when Daddy asked him if he ever played on it, he seemed to get very much flustered and said:

"'No, no! It was my father's violin. He gave it to me. It is not to be played on, nowadays. It is a rare treasure —only to look at!' But just the same, we were sure he *was* playing on it that night we happened to pass by his shack. It was quite late, and I suppose he thought no one was around. And he was playing beautifully! Only he stopped when he heard footsteps and did not go on again. So you see there must be some mystery about that violin, but I can't imagine what it is."

The puzzle was too much for all of them, and they were getting near the Hermit's shack, so the subject was dropped. During their walk, the mist of the earlier hour had developed into quite a fog which hung heavy over the gray surf and blanketed the dunes, so that it was difficult to see many feet ahead. Jack and Jill were a little worried by it and wondered whether they might lose their way going back. But Marcella cheerfully explained that that wasn't possible if they just followed the line of surf all the way back. And she knew the markings on the beach so well that she couldn't miss the turn which led to the Inn. There was an enormous old barrel on the beach right near the Inn, she explained, and you just walked along till you came to that.

They ran across the beach to the dunes between which nestled the Hermit's shack, just dimly visible through the mist. But when they got to the door and knocked there was no response, and trying the door proved that it was locked.

"Let's go around to the window and look in," suggested Jack. "Maybe he has fallen asleep and doesn't hear us." They ran around to the side of the shack where the window was and peered in. The afternoon was already waning to an early twilight, and the fog made it even darker. But they could see enough of the interior to realize there was no one within. A peep into the museum window revealed the same state of affairs there.

"That's awfully queer!" declared Marcella. "I'm sure his ankle can't be fit to walk on yet, but he must be out—and in this fog!" But Jill, remembering her success on a former occasion, was once more examining the little path that led toward the Bay. And again she made a discovery, which she excitedly called to the attention of the other two.

"Look here—both of you! There's the same footprint—and two little round holes right near each one. That must be the crutch. He's gone on his crutches the same way he did before. What shall we do?"

It was indeed a problem. What *were* they to do? This time there did not seem the urgent need to search for him that there had been before. Then the house had been wide open and there was every excuse to hunt him up, under the circumstances. Now the house was locked and the signs all pointed to the fact that he had gone out deliberately, closed and locked his door, and intended to be away for some definite time. Following him might seem like an intrusion. Yet there were the fog and his still troublesome ankle and the food they had brought for him and could not leave in the house. But more than all was the teasing fact that he had evidently taken the same path that he had on that momentous day when he had ended by nearly sinking in the marsh. Suppose the same thing had happened again? At last Marcella decided it.

"I think we had better leave the pie and biscuits in his shed back there, up on the shelf, and just follow these footprints a way and make sure he hasn't got into the marsh again. I'd never be satisfied to go back without making sure he was all right in that way."

"But won't we get lost in the fog?" demanded Jill. "It's awfully thick in toward the Bay."

"Not if we follow this little path and keep our eye on the footprints. It's still light enough to see them quite well," declared Marcella. So they placed the food in the shed and set out to follow the single footprints flanked by the two round crutch holes in the now very familiar winding path. Breathless they reached the spot where, on that memorable first day, they had come to a pause and realized that the footprints went no farther, and later had seen the cat peering in through the bushes by the marsh. But Boots was not with them now, and the footprints did not halt at this place, but went straight on, where the path curved round a cluster of cedar trees.

"He must have gone on toward the Bay," panted Marcella. And without more words they hurried along. It was not more than fifty feet farther on that the path gave another sharp turn and ended surprisingly right on the shore of the Bay, which was heavily wooded at this point. Here the fog was so dense and so close to the water that it seemed fairly to press down on the still, unrippled surface of the Bay.

But right down to the edge of the water the footsteps continued, and there they stopped, having turned neither to the right nor the left. And where they stopped on the seaweed-strewn sand was a curious, triangular mark, still visible because the tide was going out. Marcella stopped stock-still and pointed to it.

"Now I know," she gasped, winded from their hurried scramble along the path, "I know just what he's done, but I can't think why. He's gone out in his boat. Here's the mark where he pushed it off. But what *for* in such a fog as this?"

The others could not answer that question.

Chapter VI

OUT OF THE FOG

SUDDENLY Marcella had an idea. "Oh, I think maybe I know what's happened!" she announced. "He probably started out in his boat before the fog came up. You remember, it was almost sunny when we first left home. Well, he often goes out in his boat to get a few clams or oysters out of the Bay. Perhaps he wanted some very badly and thought he could get them while it was nice out. Then the fog came down, and—and he's out there now—and perhaps he can't find his way in! You don't know which way you're going when you're out on the water in a fog like this. Every direction looks just alike. Oh, I hope he won't get lost and drift away down toward the Inlet! He'd be carried out to sea and never be able to get back if he got caught in that current. It's so swift!"

They all considered the situation in a rather horrified silence. "What shall we do, then?" whispered Jack. "We—we can't leave him like this!"

"I'll tell you!" exclaimed Jill, seized with a sudden inspiration. "Maybe he's out there not so far away now. Let's all just *yell*—as loud as we can. If he hears that, he'll perhaps know which way to turn."

"Yes, we might do that," agreed Marcella, though rather dubiously. "The only trouble is that in a fog like this even sounds don't go right. They are sort of muffled. Still, I think we ought to try it. Perhaps all of us together could make a pretty loud noise. But don't let's just yell without saying anything. Let's call his name as loud as we can. Then he'll know there are some friends around, and it will be easier to understand."

Accordingly they all stood at the edge of the shore, took long breaths and shrieked, "Mr. Seymour—Mr. Seymour—*Mr. Seymour!*" again and again, till they were as hoarse as so many crows. Every little while they would stop and listen intently, trying to catch any answering shout. But the woolly gray fog gave back no reply, and what little they could see of the water was as still and unruffled as a glassy pool. At last, when they had no voices left, they stood, still and discouraged, demanding of one another what was to be done next.

"I hate to give it up," croaked Marcella hoarsely. "But we can't stay here any longer. It's getting darker and they'll all be worried about us back home. We'd better go on back and tell Daddy about this, and he can decide what's best to do." There seemed no other way that anyone could suggest, so they turned and picked their way disconsolately back along the little path, now grown almost indistinguishable in the fog, till they reached the Hermit's shack once more. And here a new surprise awaited them. Instead of the closed and empty shack they had left a while before, the light of a kerosene lamp shone out through the window, and someone was moving about inside!

"Wait!" commanded Jack, suddenly halting the other two, as he had been at the head of the procession. "Someone's in there—got in while he was away, probably. Let's just creep up to the window and peek in. And if it's someone who has no business to be there, we'll hurry right back to the Inn and get your father to come down, Marcella."

"But suppose we get caught!" shuddered Jill.

"Oh, *hush!*" whispered her brother. "Run on home, if you're afraid, and we'll follow you later!" But this challenge was too much for Jill, and she tiptoed after them without further question. Silently they crept close and ranged themselves below the little window. Then, at a sign from Jack, they cautiously raised themselves and peered in at the lighted interior of the little shack. For one long moment they clung to the window ledge; then simultaneously they dropped to the sand and whispered an incredulous query.

"Did you see what I saw?" demanded Jill in an awed undertone.

"It was the Hermit—but what was he doing?" muttered Jack.

"Of course it was he—but how did he get there—and was *that*——"

"Yes, *was* that—the *Strad?*" re-echoed Jill.

For what they had seen was simply this. The Hermit

was there, inside his own shack, safe and sound enough —and after they had imagined him struggling desperately with the fog in a lone boat out on the Bay. But what he was doing was even more astonishing than that fact. Supported by his crutches, he was standing in front of the open cabinet on the wall, and in his hands he was holding a violin—*the Stradivarius violin* —gazing at it long and lovingly! The children were too astounded to discuss it.

"Tell you what!—let's go round to the door right now—and knock—and perhaps we'll find out what it's all about," suggested Jill.

"I suppose we might as well," assented Marcella. "After all, we did come down here to bring him that pie and the biscuits. And we've spent a lot of time by the Bay trying to help him. Come on!"

They ran around to the door and rapped loudly, and they thought they could hear a surprised exclamation from inside. But, contrary to his usual custom, the Hermit did not hurry at once to admit them. There seemed to be, for the space of several seconds, a complete silence inside the hut. Then they heard the tap-tap of his crutches on the floor, and in another moment the door opened and he was peering outside in a somewhat disturbed manner. Then he recognized them standing there in the fog, and his surprise seemed great.

"Why, how did you children get here so late, and in all this fog?" he queried, and then invited them in —an invitation which they promptly accepted. Marcella explained what had brought them, earlier in the afternoon, how they had found him gone, traced his footsteps to the shore of the Bay, and then had been worried for fear he had been caught in the fog and could not find his way back, and had stood there calling and shouting to help guide him in if he were near by.

"At last we had to give it up," she ended, "but we were surprised when we passed here to see a light in the shack, so we knocked, to find out if you'd got back." She did not tell him they had peeped in the window first, for she somehow hated to have him think they had been intruding on his privacy. He seemed both amused and touched by their concern for him.

"I did go out earlier in the afternoon," he admitted, "and poked around a bit in the boat, looking for clams —and so on. And the fog did overtake me, just as you thought. So much so that I got quite confused and finally found myself near the shore, but way down, nearly half a mile nearer the Inlet. So I just moored the boat there and crossed over to the ocean side and plugged away back along the surf. I didn't hear a thing of all the shouting and was very much surprised when

I heard your knock. But won't you all sit down and rest a while?" For they had remained standing about, a trifle uneasily.

But Marcella thanked him and said they had better be getting on their way homeward before it was entirely dark, or their people at the Inn would begin to worry. She told him that they had left the biscuits and pie in the shed outside and asked how his ankle was getting on.

"It's doing very well," he assured her. "By the first of next week I'm sure I shall be able to discard the crutch and get about pretty much as usual. But thank your father and Samantha for the pie and biscuits, won't you? It's awfully kind of them to take pity on my afflictions. And come again soon." He laughed in his usual cheery fashion, and yet they thought they could detect a half-hidden uneasiness. Marcella longed to say something about the violin, but could not bring herself to mention it, for that would have revealed their unintentional spying on him through the window.

"Ask your father, if you will, Marcella, if he will be kind enough to have David get my mail next time he goes to town. No one has called for it, I think, since I had this accident." And with this he bade them good-bye and watched them scuttle away through the fog, down toward the shore. Then his door was closed and the light vanished.

They came upon the line of the surf with startling unexpectedness as it loomed dimly through the mist in the fast waning light. And keeping close together, at Marcella's command, so that they might not get separated in the fog, they hurried along the line of the creeping waves on the long mile stretch toward home. But just once they stopped, shortly after they had reached the beach and consulted together in low, agitated tones, for there was something of utter surprise that they had to confide to one another.

"Did you see that violin cabinet on the wall?" demanded Jack.

"Yes. It was shut and locked, I guess, when he let us in," supplemented Jill.

"*And it was empty!*" added Marcella in an awed voice.

"Then where was the violin?" Jack took up the questioning.

"He must have hidden it somewhere else. It wasn't anywhere around the room," declared Jill.

"He couldn't have, because he didn't move till he came straight to open the door—or we'd have heard his crutch," insisted Marcella. "And if that's so, what in the world happened to it?"

Chapter VII

AN UNLOOKED-FOR TANGLE

ALL THE WAY BACK to the Inn the three children were rather worried, anticipating a good deal of criticism from their elders because they had stayed out so late on an intensely foggy afternoon, arriving back well after dark.

"I'm certain Daddy won't like it and will hold me responsible for keeping you all out so late and perhaps worrying your father and mother," admitted Marcella when they had confided their fears to one another. "But I don't see how we could help it, because we were so worried about whether the Hermit was safe. I'll tell Daddy that, and he'll probably explain it to your folks."

"Oh, they'll understand!" declared Jack hopefully. "And anyway, it couldn't be helped, as you say."

But when they reached the Inn they found it in a stir of some excitement over a new arrival who had come in only a few moments before, and Mr. Danby merely commented to Marcella that he was glad she was back before it got too late and dark and foggy. He remarked also that the other children's parents had begun to worry, but that he had assured them that she knew her way about blindfolded and would bring them safely back before very long.

"But who is it that's just come?" asked Marcella, for the guest had evidently been shown to a room and was invisible, though David was scuttling about arranging another table in the dining room and running upstairs and downstairs with towels and room supplies. Overnight guests at that time of the year were such a novelty that Marcella was always intensely curious about them.

"Why, he's a rather young man, about twenty-five or -six, I should think. Nice sort of a chap. Says his name is—oh, bother!—I can't think what it is. You'll have to look at the register. He's down for a few days of fishing—brought a whole raft of rods and reels—though I told him the surf fishing was almost over now. Anyway, he said he had a week or so of holiday and loves to fish better than anything and had heard this was a good place, well away from everything and just right for his kind of sport. Run along now and get ready for dinner. You'll see for yourself what he's like then." And Mr. Danby turned back to his desk.

Marcella went to her room to freshen up, but first she peeped into the big hotel register on her father's desk, in which she found a record of the latest comer: Harold B. Robinson, New York.

"Not a very interesting name!" she thought disappointedly as she sped upstairs to brush her hair and change her dress for dinner. But Harold B. Robinson proved more interesting than his title and before that first evening was over had managed to grasp and hold the fascinated attention of every one of them.

The children saw him first at dinner, seated at a

small table by himself. Marcella liked his pleasant, sunny smile, his curling dark hair and twinkling eyes. She liked his voice, too, which had a musical resonant quality, as he exchanged a few remarks on the fishing possibilities with Mr. Danby, and on the likelihood of the fog clearing before the next day.

After dinner, when all gathered in the living room around the fire for a while, he brought out his rods and reels and spent an hour getting his tackle in readiness. And when that was done, strolling about the room later, he presently sat down at the piano, ran nimble fingers over the keys, then launched into the Beethoven Minuet in G and held his listeners spellbound with its haunting melody. And when they begged him for more, he passed on to another phase, rippled a few chords, and accompanying himself, sang "The Road to Mandalay," in a fashion to thrill them to their very finger tips. But more than that he would not offer, for he said he was tired and needed to get to bed early, as he planned to be up before sunrise and out for a day's surf fishing. And, smiling on them all delightfully, he said "Good-night" and went off upstairs, leaving them to wonder and discuss him at great length.

But next morning he was not about when the children left for school, and by afternoon they had practically forgotten him, in a return to their absorbed interest in the affairs of the Hermit. The fog of the previous day had completely cleared, and they had resolved to trek down the beach immediately on their return from school and call on him, taking with them his mail, which David had brought from town that morning. They had not even thought of the newcomer till they were a short distance from the Hermit's shack, when they came upon young Mr. Robinson whipping the surf with his line and making a pretty expert cast every few moments out beyond the overfall. He had two large bluefish in his basket and was intensely sunburned and seemed perfectly happy.

"Hello! where are you all going?" he greeted them breezily. But when Marcella indicated that their destination was the little shack between the dunes, she thought he looked a bit startled, though he made no comment. But it was when they reached the shack later, knocked, and found the Hermit at home, that the most surprising thing occurred. For the Hermit, contrary to his usual cheerfulness, seemed absent-minded and upset. He was hobbling about without his crutches and turned immediately to stare out of the little window at the figure of the fisherman, just to be discerned beyond the dunes, casting his line at the edge of the surf.

"Who is that man?" demanded the Hermit, before they had had a chance to say a word beyond the first greeting. "I saw you speaking to him just now. Do you know him?"

"Oh, yes. He's a Mr. Robinson who came last night to stay at the Inn," Marcella informed him. "We think he's awfully nice. He came for a week or two of fishing. But you should hear how he can play the piano—and *sing*. It was wonderful!" The Hermit drank in all this information greedily, while with a scowl between his brows he continued to stare out of the window at the unaware fisherman. His conduct struck Marcella as extremely queer. Fishermen were not unusual, even at this season of the year, on their beach, and there seemed nothing about young Mr. Robinson to cause the Hermit to be so upset. So she added, "Would you like to meet him? We can ask him to come up here. I think he'd like to see your museum." This she said as a sort of experiment, to see how the Hermit would act.

The result surprised them all. For the Hermit turned to them with an icy look and said, in a quiet but chilling voice:

"Don't ever bring him in here, if you please. I do not wish to make his acquaintance. I have a very special reason for asking this, and I do not care to explain it." He said no more and turned back again to the window. But a cold, paralyzing silence kept his visitors from making so much as a comment on his singular request. At last Marcella managed to stammer:

"Here is your mail—Mr. Seymour. David got it this morning—as you asked." And this brought about another change in the Hermit's manner. Softening immediately, he became again the cheery, courteous host that they had always found him.

"Thanks a lot!" he exclaimed. "You children have certainly saved my life in more ways than one. I'd be awfully glad if you could manage to bring down the mail as often as possible, as I don't expect to be able to get up to town for some time yet. And here's a list of the groceries and things I'll need, if your father will be so good as to order them for me. I don't know how I'll ever be able to thank you all for helping me over this difficult time." His manner was so cordial that the children could hardly believe they had heard that icy note in his voice only a moment or so before. After some further conversation they left, saying they were going to hunt for old bottles on their way up the beach. When they went out again, the fisherman had disappeared, nor did they catch sight of him again all the way back.

"I can't understand it!" cried Marcella when they were out of sight of the shack. "I never heard him speak like that before. What *do* you suppose was the matter?"

"Something wrong with Mr. Harold B. Robinson, all right!" declared Jack solemnly. "You can just see that the Hermit hates the sight of him."

"But why should he?" demanded Jill hotly. "That Mr. Robinson only got here last night. The Hermit doesn't even know him, probably. I don't see how anyone can hate Mr. Robinson. I think he's awfully nice. And he plays and sings beautifully."

"*That* doesn't prove anything!" declared Jack scornfully. "But there's just one thing that strikes me as —well, queer. Just about the same time that the Hermit gets all upset about something or other—we don't know what—this new person turns up. Now that wouldn't be at all strange ordinarily, but the very first day he's here we find the Hermit glaring at him out of the window as if he couldn't stand the sight of him. And when we offer to bring this new man in, the Hermit nearly has a fit, and tells us he never wants to see him—or something like that. So *that* proves there must be some reason—and that the Hermit must know him. And yet I can't think why!"

And, as usual, it was Jill who had a brilliant inspiration. She halted them all, stood stock-still and half whispered:

"Listen—I'm *sure* I'm right. It just came to me. Mr. Robinson is a *detective!* He's here in disguise to spy on the Hermit for some reason or other. He's *watching* him! And the Hermit must know it, and that's why he doesn't want him around or want us to bring Mr. Robinson to see him. Don't you see it all now?" The other two stared at her spellbound for a moment. Then Jack said gravely:

"But if that's so, it must mean that the Hermit has done something wrong—if they've gotten somebody to watch him." And at this horrifying thought, Marcella burst out:

"It isn't so! It isn't—it *isn't!* The Hermit never did anything wrong. I'll never believe it. He's too nice. And besides, we've known him for years and years. He's lived here a long time. How *could* he do anything wrong when he just lives here all by himself and never goes anywhere hardly ever?"

"Well, maybe they only *think* he's done something wrong and he really hasn't—and they're watching the wrong person," offered Jill, anxious not to give up her detective theory.

"That might be, too," agreed Jack. "Perhaps that's what it is. They're watching the wrong person—and that detective is all on the wrong scent. Tell you what —let's take to watching Mr. Robinson—if he *is* a detective—and see if we can guess, from the way he acts, what he's trying to do. Then we might be more able to help the Hermit—if he needs any help."

"I'm going to have a talk with Daddy," announced Marcella, "and tell him all about the queer things that have happened and ask him what *he* thinks about it all."

"You can't tell him *everything*," Jill reminded her, "because, don't you remember, the Hermit asked us not to say anything about how we found him in the marsh that first day? You'll have to leave all that out."

"That's so!" sighed Marcella. "I didn't think of it. That makes it a lot harder. I've already told Dad how his violin seemed to have disappeared, but I haven't had a chance to tell him what's happened since. But unless I can tell him the whole thing, it doesn't make much sense. Oh, I *wish* people wouldn't ask you not to say anything about the things you want most to talk about!" she ended impatiently.

They had come to no conclusion, when they reached the Inn, as to what they had best do, and events that evening did not help to straighten matters out but only threw them into worse confusion. For, after the evening meal, when all had gathered in the living room, Mr. Robinson strolled in and sat down near the open fire to smoke his pipe in company with the two other men. The children were busy with their lessons at a table not far away, but they had their ears wide open for any conversation that might interest them. And, before the conversation at the fireside ended, they had their reward. For young Mr. Robinson, turning to Mr. Danby, inquired casually:

"There's a very curious little shack about a mile down the beach, I noticed today. Rather interesting-looking old chap was working around outside—hobbled a bit as if he were lame. I was going over to speak to him, but he suddenly darted inside and shut the door and didn't come out again. Who is he, anyway? He looked sort of interesting."

"Oh, he is—he is!" agreed Mr. Danby, and launched into a long account of the Hermit and his quaint museum, while Mr. Robinson listened with absorbed attention. And the children, apparently intent on their arithmetic, squirmed with apprehension at all the information that was being handed out so freely to this possible "detective"—information that might help to wreck their hermit's happiness, for all they knew.

"But there's one thing he has that you certainly ought to see," ended Mr. Danby in a burst of enthusiasm. And Marcella knew instantly that her father was going to mention the Stradivarius violin, about which there now was so much mystery. And somehow, in her loyalty to the Hermit, she felt that this was precisely the thing Mr. Robinson ought *not* to hear about. But how was she going to stop her father now, with the words almost on his lips? She took a sudden desperate resolve. With one sweep of her arm she knocked the big inkwell off the table and upside-down straight into her lap!

A loud outcry from all the children greeted the apparent accident and in the commotion that followed, with David and Samantha having to be summoned to help clear up the mess, the subject of the Hermit was quite forgotten, nor was it resumed when quiet and order had been restored. And when Marcella came downstairs to finish her lessons after having changed her dress, Mr. Robinson was sitting at the piano, playing something soft and dreamy, and later added a song or two in his beautiful tenor voice. After which he bade them all a friendly good-night and went off to bed.

But before she herself slept, Marcella had had a short interview with her father, in which she begged him not to mention the violin to the newcomer. And when Mr. Danby had demanded an astonished, "Why not?" she could only tell him what had happened that afternoon, and add:

"I think the Hermit doesn't like him, but we can't guess why. And we've known the Hermit so long—and he's such a friend—it doesn't seem fair to tell everything we know about him to Mr. Robinson. He may be an enemy of the Hermit's—we can't tell. Anyhow, don't say anything more about it all to Mr. Robinson, will you—*will you*, Daddy?"

She was so earnest in her appeal that her father could not deny her request, though he protested:

"It all seems rather absurd to me, Marcella. And you may have been mistaken about how the Hermit felt—or he may have mistaken Mr. Robinson for someone else. But, anyhow, it's of no great importance. Mr. Robinson only expects to be here a few days, and he probably doesn't care one way or the other about Herbert Seymour's affairs. He only asked out of idle curiosity. But if it'll keep you happy, I promise not to say anything more about our neighbor! Now are you satisfied, Honeybird?"

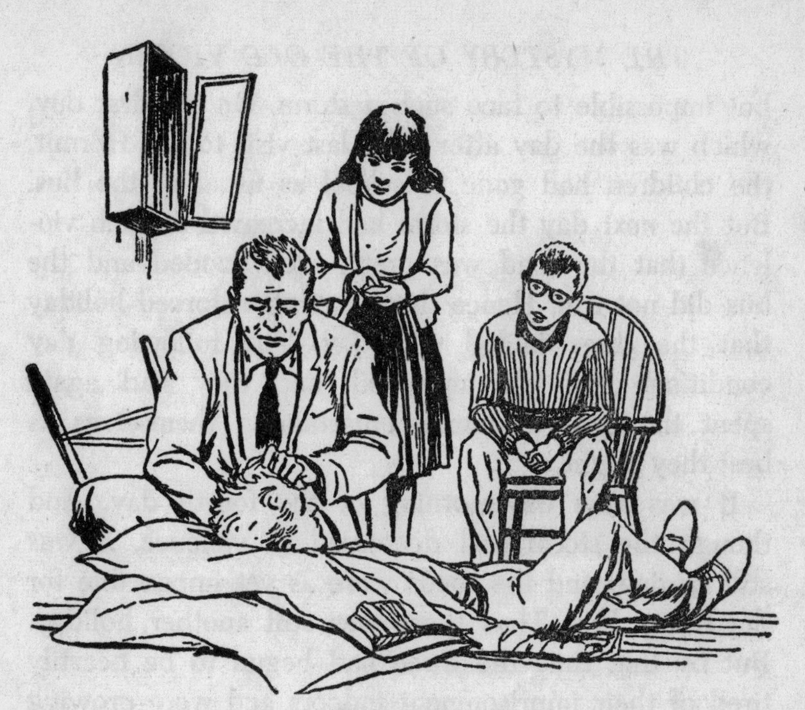

Chapter VIII

CROSSWORD PUZZLES—AND CATASTROPHE

IT HAD BEEN RAINING for several days. No ordinary rain, but a terrific downpour, accompanied by howling winds and blasts of sand from the beach. It was all but impossible to face such a storm. On the first day, which was the day after their last visit to the Hermit, the children had gone to school as usual in the bus. But the next day the storm had increased to such violence that the road was pretty well flooded and the bus did not run. Hence there was an enforced holiday that the three hailed with joy. The following day conditions had not improved, and they had again spent the time at home, entertaining themselves as best they might.

It was now the morning of the fourth day. And though the storm had decreased in violence, it was still raining, and the roads were as yet impassable for the heavy bus. Thus there was still another holiday. But by that time the three had begun to be heartily tired of their imprisonment indoors and were growing restless and rather noisy, especially Jack and Jill. Their indoor romping had begun to get on the nerves of Mr. Burdick to such an extent that Mr. Danby took Marcella aside and warned her:

"You'll have to try and think of something to do to keep those two more quiet, my dear. Their father is beginning to be very much upset. See if you can't plan something that will keep them from tearing up and down stairs and shouting and quarreling with each other. Take them to your room and play some games

—or *something*—or Mr. Burdick will be ill again. I wish I could turn you all out of doors, but it's still too stormy."

So Marcella had herded the noisy youngsters into her own room and, as they had long since played every game they could think of over and over again, suggested in desperation:

"Let's do some of those crossword puzzles you were working on that day you came. You always told me you'd show me how to do them, but somehow we've never got at it, 'cause we had so many other things to do. I think I'd like them."

The other two fell upon the idea with enthusiasm and got out their books, which they had not looked at since the first evening at the Inn. Each one began to do a puzzle in his or her own book. Marcella went back and forth between them, learning quickly the trick of it and, as she was good in spelling, proving remarkably clever at working out the words. She was leaning over Jack and puzzling out a corner when Jill called:

"Here's one, Marcella, that you ought to know—'A kind of fish'! There are four letters, and the last one is 's.' I can't seem to think of any that ends with 's.' "

" 'Bass,' " cried Marcella promptly. Jill inserted the

letters and added, "Speaking of fish—where's our Mr. Robinson all this time? We don't see much of him except at meals."

"Oh, he's around, but I guess he isn't getting much fishing done—in *this* weather," answered Marcella, wrestling with a definition in Jack's book which called for "things to take hold of." "I think it must be 'handles,' Jack. It's seven letters. He wanders around downstairs and plays solitaire and smokes and reads. Once in a while he plays the piano. And then he wraps up in his oilskins and goes out a lot on the beach. He told Daddy he liked to be right out in the storm and feel it shove him around. But Daddy thinks it's queer he hasn't got discouraged and gone home. Most of them do in such a bad storm as this—if it lasts long."

"I wonder where he goes when he goes out?" cried Jill, suddenly throwing down her pencil and bending her mind to the new problem. "Do you suppose he ever gets down as far as the Hermit's?"

"Yes, and talking about the Hermit—what's been happening to him in all this storm?" demanded Jack. "He's been left there all by himself, and maybe his food has been used up and he's lame still and can't get around much. I just wonder what *he's* doing?"

"Well, don't worry about him—at least, not about his food and that sort of thing. Daddy sent down a lot of meat and fresh vegetables that first day with David, when it wasn't so bad. The Hermit has always told us that he has a special supply of canned things and crackers that he keeps put away for an emergency just like this. He said he had enough to live on for a week or so, even if no one came near him. So that's all right—and his house is awfully strong. It couldn't get damaged by wind and rain. But I do wonder if any queer things have happened to him since—things like what were going on lately. I've sort of been thinking of him all the time and wondering if there were any more trouble."

No one could answer this question, so they presently went back to their crossword puzzles.

"Here's a queer one," presently announced Jill. "Eleven letters, and it's called, 'a very disastrous happening.' It begins with 'ca' and ends with 'e.' But I can't get any of the other letters."

"'Calamity'!" suggested Jack, but was hooted at by his sister for offering a word that didn't have sufficient letters and ended in the wrong letter. No one could think of any other. They were just about to hunt up the dictionary when Marcella heard her father calling her from below. She hurried down to him.

"I've just had a message from a coastguard," said Mr. Danby, "who was on his way up the beach on fog patrol. He said that as he was passing the Hermit's shack he noticed something white fluttering from one of the windows and went up to see if anything was wrong. There was a white handkerchief caught between the window and the sill, and it looked as if it had been put there to attract attention. But he knocked on the door, and no one came, and the door was locked. He even looked in the window, but could not see anyone inside. He doesn't know what it all means, but thought he'd better stop and tell me, as I know Mr. Seymour better than anyone else and would probably want to do something about it. The coastguard himself—it was Bainbridge, Number Two man at the next station—had to hurry on, as he was late and has still a mile further to go."

"Oh, the poor Hermit!" cried Marcella anxiously. "Do you suppose some awful thing could have happened to him, Dad?"

"No, probably nothing very awful, but he may be in some difficulty that we can help him out of. He must be, or he wouldn't have hung out that signal. I told him a long time ago that if he ever wanted anything special, or needed any help, to hang out a white cloth of some kind and the coastguards would see it and let me know. If there were only a road down to his shack it would be different. But he's absolutely cut off from communication except by the beach. Anyhow, I'm going down there at once. And as it seems to have stopped storming, I propose to take you and the other youngsters with me, if their parents will let them go. Be a good thing for you to get some fresh air and work off steam trotting down the beach. And it can't hurt any of you if you're well wrapped up."

Ten minutes later the four of them were trudging down the beach, clad in boots and slickers. And Mr. Danby carried along some emergency remedies, in case the Hermit had met with a fresh accident. It was a new experience for the Burdick children—this tramp along the wreckage-strewn shore, dodging great waves in which huge logs and débris were still being cast up, wading through seas of froth and foam, battling the wind and tasting the salt spray on their lips. On the beach the flotsam and jetsam included every manner of article of which one could think. Jill picked up an enormous sodden Teddy bear and a wax head that looked as if it might have been part of a show-window figure. Jack found innumerable bottles that intrigued him, but Mr. Danby warned them that it was foolish to lug along everything they saw to which they might take a fancy. If they liked they could collect them on the way back. Only Marcella, to whom such storms were no novelty, did not burden herself with anything. It had to be a rare and unusual treasure that could attract her. Besides, she was too much worried over what might have happened to the Hermit to be interested today in "beach-combing," as Mr. Danby called it.

At last they came in sight of the Hermit's shack. It was still closed, and no one was about. The white handkerchief fluttered from the window, as the coast-guard had described. Mr. Danby knocked at the door loudly and waited, but received no reply. Then he went to the window and examined the handkerchief that was fastened there. It had been held in its place by the sash, and a little corner of it was on the inside, where the window had been lowered on it.

"I don't believe that window is fastened on the inside," announced Mr. Danby. "Anyhow, I'm going to take a chance and raise it and get in this way. You children stay outside till I do a bit of exploring. Then I'll let you in through the door." He tried the sash and found, as he had thought, that it would open, inserted a leg inside, and was about to follow with the rest of his body—when he suddenly drew back, pulled his leg out, and cried out: "Good gracious!—what's all this?"

"What's the matter, Daddy?" cried Marcella in alarm. "What did you see?"

"It isn't what I *saw*—it's what I *felt!*" exclaimed Mr. Danby, mopping his face with his handkerchief. "When I put my foot down in there I stepped on something soft—a human body!" He turned and stuck his head in the open window and peered about. Then quickly he drew his head back.

"Yes, it's he—the Hermit—lying there right under the window! Goodness knows how long he's been there. He's hurt—badly, I'm afraid. Let me get in again at once." The window was rather high. Getting in without hurting the Hermit beneath on the floor was difficult, but Mr. Danby finally accomplished it, bent down out of sight for a long moment, then went over and unfastened the door.

"Come in very softly," he bade the children. "You may be able to help me. He's lying there unconscious. His head is cut, but I think we'll be able to bring him round all right. Do just as I tell you and don't ask any unnecessary questions till this is over."

"Daddy," whispered Marcella suddenly, "*look*—just a moment—at this room! It's awfully upset. What can have happened?"

It did indeed look as if it had been the scene of a dreadful struggle. Furniture was overturned, a tablecloth had been dragged from the little table, bringing with it plates and cups and the remains of a meal; one of the chairs was broken, even the pictures had been dragged off the walls or knocked askew. Confusion was everywhere, and on the corner of a shelf near the window was a streak of blood. "Must have hit his head there as he fell," indicated Mr. Danby. "Something pretty rough has been going on here."

Marcella suddenly turned her eyes to the violin case on the wall, where for so long now the Stradivarius had not hung. The case door was wrenched open and hung by one hinge. But otherwise it appeared intact. Only no violin was visible.

Mr. Danby, however, gave no further thought to the condition of the room, but set about doing what he could to bring the Hermit back to consciousness. He sent Jack to get a glass of fresh water at the pump, Marcella to hunt up a towel and spoon, and Jill to find some pillows from the couch to put under his head. Then he proceeded to pour a dose of aromatic ammonia through the half-open lips and wipe the cut on the temples with a towel and fresh water.

They had just been rewarded by a flutter of eyelids and a deep-drawn sigh from the Hermit when they were startled by a loud knock at the door!

Chapter IX

WHO WAS AT THE DOOR?

"Go see who that is, Marcella," ordered Mr. Danby, "and tell whoever it is, unless it's the coastguard, that we're pretty busy just now."

Marcella hastened to obey, snapped the lock, and

opened the door—and confronted Mr. Harold B. Robinson, in his slicker and boots.

"Oh—er—Daddy!" she stammered. "It's *Mr. Robinson!*"

"I was on my way over to the beach," interrupted that young man, "and heard voices in here and thought I'd stop and ask if anything were wrong. I hope I'm not intruding but I had a reason for asking this."

While he was speaking he could not help but see the figure on the floor in the room and the signs of struggle all about the place. "Then there *has* been trouble," he added. "I thought so!" Mr. Danby, still busy with the Hermit, replied:

"Since you're here, Mr. Robinson, you might help us get him to the couch. He'll rest easier there, and I think he's coming back to consciousness." The Hermit, indeed, was groaning softly and muttering indistinguishable words.

Mr. Robinson assented gladly. Together they lifted him by the shoulders and feet, carried him to the couch, and arranged him comfortably. "I think I'd better bind up his head next," decided Mr. Danby. "He's lost a lot of blood from that cut on his forehead and will lose more if it isn't seen to. Get a basin of fresh water, Marcella. And you, Jack, please unroll that gauze bandage and get me the absorbent cotton I brought. Lucky I thought of those things!"

Deftly Mr. Danby cleansed the cut and wound the bandage round and round the Hermit's head. He was just fastening it when the Hermit startled everyone by suddenly exclaiming out loud:

"Solange—*Solange!*—oh, bring him back!—the *boy!* it was all—mistake——" Then he relapsed again into semiconsciousness. The other occupants of the room stared at one another in amazement. To whom could he be calling?

"His mind is wandering," declared Mr. Danby. "He's only half-conscious. He'll come to himself in a little while. Hold up his head a bit, if you will, Mr. Robinson, while I try to give him some more aromatic ammonia." Mr. Robinson made haste to do as he had been asked, but murmured to Mr. Danby:

"Who is he calling to, do you know? The name —Solange—is singular!"

"Haven't the slightest idea—never heard it before," said Mr. Danby. "There's a good deal of mystery about him. He's lived here for years, but no one knows anything about his earlier life or where he came from. Must be something to do with that. Look!—his eyes are opening. He's coming to himself at last!"

The Hermit, having swallowed Mr. Danby's dose,

coughed, opened his eyes, stared about, struggled to one elbow and cried out:

"My violin—my Strad!—he took it—he fought me for it!—he got away——" And then, suddenly recognizing Mr. Danby, "Oh—how did you get here?—I'm hurt, I think—— But you—*you!*—how dare you come back here when you stole my Strad? How *dare* you?" This last was to Mr. Robinson, who had been behind him, holding his head, and whom he had just caught sight of. Mr. Danby and the children turned their amazed faces toward Mr. Robinson, who, however, calmly replied:

"You're mistaken, sir. I didn't steal your Strad. But I happen to have met with the person who *did*, just a little while ago. And for reasons which I'll explain later I took it forcibly away from him and came back here to return it to you. It's right outside the door. I left it there when I came in. Wait a moment and I'll get it!"

It was the tensest moment Marcella had ever known. Mr. Robinson went to the door, opened it, and drew in a bulky bundle wrapped in a worn shawl. Unwinding the folds of it, he drew out the lost Stradivarius, unharmed, and laid it in the Hermit's outstretched hands, saying:

"Here you are, sir! And it may interest you to know

that I gave the thief a good trouncing and sent him off down the Bay with some marks to remember both of us by!"

The Hermit seemed still too dazed to take it all in. He stared at the violin. Then he stared at the young man, and at last managed to stammer:

"I—I thank you—and I—apologize—for my blunder. It was a young man—like you—in height—and dark hair. That was all I knew. But who are you? I do not think I know your name."

The young man did not answer in words, but he did a strange thing. He took up the violin and its bow, tucked the instrument under his chin, and looking at the Hermit, asked: "Do you happen to recognize this?" And from the strings there came a low, haunting melody like a lullaby or cradle song, but unfamiliar to any of his listeners—save one. For after the first few notes, the Hermit struggled to his elbow, stared wildly at the player, and gasped:

"No, no—no! —*It can't be!*"

"Yes," said the young man very gently, "it *is!*"

Chapter X

THE END OF THE MYSTERY

IN THE TENSE MOMENT that followed these strange remarks, the young man dropped down beside the Hermit on the couch and took both his hands in his own.

"You guessed it—but not before I did—*Father!*" was all he said, but it left the Hermit apparently stunned, and the other four listeners speechless. It was Mr. Danby who first recovered himself.

"I see that something very unforeseen has occurred here," he said, "and I'm sure that you two would prefer to be left alone for a while. I suggest that I take the children and go back to the Inn. This afternoon I'll come back with David and another strong man and a stretcher. I think it would be a good thing for Mr. Seymour to rest up a few days at the Inn, where we can take good care of him and make him comfortable, and he won't have to be alone while he's recovering from this—accident. Between us all we can get him there comfortably. Do you both agree?"

The Hermit still looked almost too dazed to reply, but after a moment's thought nodded assent, and Mr. Robinson agreed that the plan was excellent. And so, much to the children's disappointment, the four of them took their departure.

"I don't understand it!" cried Marcella when they were on the beach again, facing the heavy northeast gale. "What is it all about, Daddy?"

"I don't understand it either," said Mr. Danby, shouting against the wind, "except that we've just seen the reunion of a father and son—somehow or other. But this is no time to discuss it. We can't shout like this all the way home. Save your breath for the journey. No doubt we'll hear all about it later!" And with that the children had to be content.

And after the storm a calm! Clear, crisp, marvelous November weather such as is found only on the seashore at that season, filled with the sweet scent of the pines and the tang of the sea. It was the day after the exciting event. And the three children, having gone back to school that morning, were now, in the late afternoon, returning along the beach from the Hermit's shack. They had gone to see if all were secure. They had found the heavy shutters closed tightly over the windows, the door locked, and no footprints around. For the Hermit had been brought to the Inn that afternoon, as Mr. Danby had planned, and had been resting comfortably in his room. But both he and Mr. Robinson had been practically invisible ever since.

"When do you think we're going to see them both again—and hear all about it?" demanded Jill impatiently.

"Maybe you aren't *ever* going to hear about it!

Maybe they don't intend to tell!" was Jack's not too soothing suggestion.

"Daddy said," remarked Marcella, "that the Hermit wasn't seriously hurt in the head, only a cut, and that it's healing nicely. He felt very weak. The shock upset him, but he'll be all right pretty soon. So maybe we will see him down in a day or two. And I'm sure he isn't going to keep us guessing all the rest of our lives."

Marcella was nearer the truth than she knew. For that very evening, after dinner, the unexpected happened. Mr. Burdick had retired early, as he usually did, and Mrs. Burdick was reading to him in their room upstairs. Only Mr. Danby and the three children were sitting about the open fire in the living room when they heard steps on the stair outside. In another moment the Hermit entered the room, escorted by young Mr. Robinson. The Hermit carried his beloved Stradivarius violin in his hand.

"May we come in?" he asked in a weak but cheery voice. "I feel a great deal better and am desperately tired of staying upstairs away from everyone but this young man. Guess he's tired of it too! So if you'll let us sit down here with you a while, perhaps we can have a chat and clear things up a bit. You must have thought I've been living behind a veil of mystery these last few days!"

They sat him down in the easiest chair, where he rested with the injured foot on a stool, his head still bandaged, and the violin lying across his knees. The young man drew up a chair near by for himself. There was a deep, expectant silence.

"Well, you might as well know it all now," said the Hermit, smiling a little. "I wonder where I'd best begin. I've lived a long time in this region, and you've known what my life has been here. But I know, too, that you must have always felt that there was some mystery about me—some things that I have never explained. And you were right. There were. And I'm going to start at the beginning—and explain them from there!" He settled himself more comfortably in his chair and went on:

"I'll have to confess at the very beginning that 'Herbert Seymour' is not my right name. Why I assumed it, I'll tell you later. But I was born 'Charles Bainbridge' and am the son of the famous Hector Bainbridge, who was for years one of the greatest violinists of this country. But perhaps none of you have ever heard of him."

"Well, *I* have," smiled Mr. Danby. "I used to hear

my father, who loved music very much, speak of having heard him give concerts."

"I don't doubt it," agreed the Hermit. "Anyone who was interested in music at that time would have known him. I was his only child, and I seem to have inherited at least some of his wonderful gift. At the age of twenty-two I myself became a violinist, giving concerts everywhere. At the end of my first public concert, which was more of a success than anyone had dreamed it would be, my father presented me with his wonderful Stradivarius violin and announced that he would retire from public life. He did so, but died a few years later. I grew to love this marvelous old violin as much as he had, and could not have given a concert without it.

"Now I shall have to tell you a little about my personal affairs. While I was giving a series of European concerts, I met in France a beautiful young woman, Solange Dumaire. We fell very much in love with each other, and before I left Europe to return to America we were married and I brought her back with me. We were very happy for a time—or at least I was—but two things greatly troubled my wife. She was homesick and longed to return to Paris. And she hated the life we had to lead, traveling about from city to city, giving concerts, with no settled home of our own. When our son was born, Harold Bainbridge, she vowed that he should never be encouraged to follow a musical career.

"But you can't stifle an inherited love for music as strong as that child had. When he could scarcely more than toddle, he would come stumbling to me when his mother was not around and sit listening spellbound while I practised. Sometimes, as he grew a little older, he would take my violin and scrape away on it till he had extracted a tune, or stand by the piano picking out the notes of a song by ear. He had a pretty voice, too, and was singing all day long. I never encouraged him in the music, since his mother did not wish it, but it made me feel very sorry that so evident a talent should be neglected.

"But as the years went by his mother had been growing more unhappy and discontented, and at last an incident happened that brought matters to a head. She came unexpectedly one day upon our little son, who had taken up my violin where I had left it, playing away by ear, and in a quite surprising fashion. I did not happen to be there at the time. But when I returned, some hours later, I found that my wife and son had both gone away, leaving only a letter for me.

The letter told me what my wife had discovered about the boy, and said that she was going away with little Harold, to disappear from my life and bring the boy up far away from any musical influence. She begged me not to try to trace them. She was quite independently well off, so had no need of my support.

"I can scarcely tell you what that terrible discovery did to me. I had loved my wife dearly and adored our little son. My desperate search for them was unsuccessful. Beyond that I could not think what I would do. I had no heart for anything, and life seemed a blank."

He sighed deeply and stared into the fire for a long moment. No one of his audience spoke a word. The children felt too tense almost to draw a breath. Presently he went on:

"I finished my concert season, but I felt that I was playing without inspiration or interest. Then I made a resolve. I was sick of music. I would play no more. I would close this chapter in my life and go away somewhere myself and begin a new one. I had made a great deal of money with my music and also had some that my father left me. But I was very well known. I knew I could go nowhere under my own name without embarrassing questions and constant reminders of the past. So I set my affairs in order, assumed the name—chosen quite at random—of 'Herbert Seymour'—and sailed for the Far East. I took no reminder of my old life with me except my beloved Stradivarius, from which I could not bring myself to part. But it was a long time before I ever played on it again.

"Finally, I grew weary at last of travel and seeing strange countries and longed to come back to America. But not to the old life—never *that* again! I wanted most of all to find some spot that was well away from crowds and all the hectic rush and roar of cities—some place near the sea where I could lead a simple and uneventful life and have some interest that was not music, but that would fill my days and keep me occupied. I found it at last, after some months of searching about, down on this lonely strip of beach. I bought the land, built my simple little shack with my own hands, and settled down. I never heard from my wife and child again. I had always hoped to stumble across them possibly in my travels, but I never did. They too seemed to have dropped out of the world they had known, as completely as I had.

"That is my story, up to very recent date. You all know how I have lived these last ten or fifteen years on this beach. There is just one other phase of it that I haven't mentioned. That concerns my violin. In the years while I was still playing for concerts, I had once a very curious interview. At the end of one of my concerts, an elderly man came to me and asked to be allowed to examine my Stradivarius violin. When he handed it back to me, to my astonishment, he said:

"'I see it is the one called *Rossignol.* I must tell you that that instrument belongs to *me!*' (I must explain here, in case you don't happen to know it, that Anton Stradivari's most famous violins were all named. This one is French for *Nightingale.* You can see it yourself, very faintly—right here on the instrument.) Of course, I asked him to explain his strange claim. He told me, then, that his name was Antonio Giotto, and his family was an ancient one in Ravenna, Italy. He said that this violin had been in his family since the day it was finished by its maker. But that fifty years or so ago it had been stolen or disappeared from their villa in Ravenna, and he had been trying ever since to trace it. He had just recently come to America and, hearing that I used a Stradivarius violin, he had asked to see it, scarcely hoping it could be the one he was searching for. I asked him what papers he had to prove it, and he said that unfortunately there had been a serious fire in his villa several years before, and all papers and documents relating to the violin had been destroyed. But he begged me to take his word for it. He even offered to buy it, and mentioned a sum that was hundreds of dollars short of what my father had paid for it, but he said it was all he had.

"I was sorely puzzled about it, for he seemed so genuine. But I told him I would have to think it over. Meanwhile I went to the firm from which my father had bought it to inquire about how it had come into *their* possession. They assured me that they knew the entire history of my *Rossignol,* traced back its ownership for a couple of hundred years most satisfactorily, and also made inquiries abroad concerning Mr. Antonio Giotto. They found him to be entirely unknown in Ravenna, with no sign of a villa there or any even remote connection. We decided that he was either an impostor or else was sort of 'off' on the subject and really imagined the instrument to be his. At any rate, I need have no further worry about my right to keep it.

"The old man followed me about for quite a long while, begging almost piteously to be allowed to buy back his violin. I did not really shake him off till I myself made the change in my name and life and disappeared from the musical world. After that, of course, I never saw him again. In all my later travels no one even knew I possessed a violin, as I never used it. But after I was settled here, I felt that I should like to be able to look at it, at least. No one about here would be likely to connect me with the former Charles Bainbridge, after all these years. So I made the strong and durable case with the glass front, fastened it to the wall, and hung my precious violin where I could look at it. Sometimes, late at night, when no one was about, I would take out my Strad and play. It was a rare treat for me, but one I dared not indulge in too often, for I did not want anyone to suspect my past. I hardly think anyone about here ever guessed that I could play the instrument."

"*We* did—Daddy and I," offered Marcella shyly. "We heard you late one summer night when we were passing—but you stopped right away."

"Ah, then you were most tactful not to mention it!" smiled the Hermit at them. "But I must hurry on and finish my story. About a month or so ago I was startled to read in the newspaper that a young man who called himself 'Tony Giotto,' announced that he had come to this country commissioned by a wealthy nobleman in Italy, to procure for him two or three Stradivarius violins. And he asked anyone who possessed such violins or knew of those who did possess them to communicate with him. So, I thought, here is the old game again—only this time it must be the son—or grandson. Perhaps he too thinks my *Rossignol* is his family property and is trying once more to get hold of it. However, it did not worry me, as I was too far away and unknown now, to have my instrument traced. And yet—as events proved, I was mistaken.

"I awoke one night—it was the night just before my accident—to realize that someone was in the room. It was warm, and I had left the front door standing open, as I often do. Looking over from my couch I saw the figure of a man—he seemed young and slight, with dark hair, standing before the case on the wall and examining the violin through the glass with a pocket electric torch. The case, as you know, I always keep locked. I must have startled him for he darted out of the door and was off like the wind.

"I tumbled out of bed and was after him, over toward the Bay. But he was too quick for me. When I got to the shore I heard a motorboat chugging away in the darkness. I went back to the shack, but there was no more sleep for me that night. I knew that I could not be mistaken. A 'Giotto' was once more on the trail of my violin. So, as I had long ago arranged for such an emergency, I opened a secret door in the cabinet which I had made when first I built it, put the violin inside this unknown compartment and locked it. No one would have dreamed any such place existed. The cabinet simply looks empty. The opening is in the back wall—built right into the wall of the shack itself."

"Golly!" cried Jack, unable to repress his excitement. "That explains a whole lot of things we were puzzled about!"

"Yes, I expect it does," the Hermit nodded to him. "I knew the violin was safe there, but I was furious that my home had been invaded and was determined to catch the fellow if possible. Early that next morning, as I was lying awake watching, I thought I heard a rustling and noises in the bushes that might be the same fellow coming back. I'm sure now I was mistaken. But I got up in the dark and dressed and hurried out toward the Bay. I turned in at that place near the marsh, caught my foot in a vine, and stumbled and wrenched my ankle so that I thought it was broken. Nevertheless, I dragged myself on, following that imaginary rustling. Before I knew it I was into the marsh, floundering about and terribly hampered by my ankle.

I was near enough to that bush to catch hold of it, but the bog was steadily sucking me downward. And I owe my life to you children, who came along and rescued me just in the nick of time."

At this revelation, Mr. Danby looked so completely stunned that the Hermit was forced to laugh as he explained: "Yes, they actually did! But I was so horribly afraid that if I let it be generally known it might lead to the discovery of my secret. I made the children promise they would not tell that part of the adventure. And they've proved they're a loyal trio—bless their hearts!

"But from that day on, my life has been a continuous misery, never knowing when there might be another visit from this hateful Giotto person. During that afternoon of the fog I felt sure he might try it again—come across the Bay in a motorboat, perhaps, so I took my own rowboat and prowled about the shore, hoping to cut him off if he did. I managed to get lost myself later, when the fog grew so thick, and got back to the shack, as I explained to you children. But then I was so worried for fear he might have gotten in during my absence and somehow discovered my hiding-place that I had to open the cabinet and see that it was all secure. And while I had it in my hands I heard a knock at the door and, before I answered it, quickly secreted the thing behind the hidden door. Then I found it was you children again."

"Did you think, sir," interrupted Jack, "the next morning, when Mr. Robinson here was fishing on the beach that *he* was this Giotto man? You told us, do you remember, never to bring him to your shack."

"Yes," admitted the Hermit, "I'm ashamed to say I did. But I wasn't so much to blame, for both of them are tall and slim and dark, and I could not see this Giotto very well that night he got in. His face was always in the shadow. I thought then that he had gone to the hotel and was posing as a fisherman, just to get at me in another way.

"Then came the big storm, and I was pretty well cut off from the world for a while, except for an occasional passing coastguard. But I was less worried about being molested at that time, as I was sure no stranger would venture down the beach or across the Bay in such a terrific near-hurricane. But I was mistaken. For that last day, when the wind and rain had let up a bit, I thought I would go over to the Bay with a little sand-sled and drag back some firewood. When I got there, I was stunned to see a strange motorboat anchored right off the shore. It seemed to be empty, so I just turned and got back to the house as fast as I could. I wasn't a moment too soon, for there was Giotto just in the act of wrenching off the glass door of the violin cabinet!

"I hardly remember what happened next, except that I sprang at him, and we had a terrible struggle. He was younger than I and I don't know what might have happened, but suddenly he stopped, threw me from him with such force that I hit my head in falling. Then he came over to me, where I lay unable to get up, for the fall and blow had stunned me. I heard him hiss at me, 'Tell me where that Strad is —or I finish you!' And I remember thinking, 'After all, life is more precious than even a violin. I'll let him take it—but I'll have it traced later—even if I have to tell my secret in the end!' So I pointed to the case and muttered, 'Door at back!' And after that I did not know any more.

"He must have found the opening, taken the Strad, and carefully closed the inner door. When I came to, the place was empty. I had only strength enough to drag myself near the window and somehow manage to get my handkerchief caught outside so that a coast-guard might see it. Then I lost consciousness again. You know what happened after that. Now I've talked enough. The rest of the story I'll let this young man here tell. It's rather wonderful to me—the part he's concerned with!" The Hermit sat back with a sigh of released tension and smiled at Mr. Harold B. Robinson, "Go ahead, son!"

They all looked over at young Mr. Robinson. "Here goes!" he began. "As you've probably guessed, I'm that little son of Charles Bainbridge—the violinist, and my name isn't 'Harold B. Robinson,' either. But it really *is*, as a matter of fact—only turned around a bit. I was named 'Harold Robinson Bainbridge' originally. But when my mother took me away to France, she called herself 'Robinson,' which had been her own mother's family name, and simply turned mine around. I grew up thinking I'd always been Harold Robinson.

"My mother was not happy in France after all. She very soon left and went to England, where she put me in a good school to be well instructed—in everything except music! I was so young when we left America that I soon forgot practically everything about my life there—even my father. Only one thing remained with me—the memory of music and trying to play on a violin and a lovely little tune that someone used to play for me. I never forgot that tune. You heard me play it the other day. It was a little cradle song that my father had composed especially for me and used to play for me occasionally—after I had been put to bed. But I didn't know that—till years later.

"As I grew older, I begged my mother to let me have music lessons, but she would not hear of it, nor would she tell me why. But I just felt that she didn't understand—I couldn't live without it, so I spent all my allowance and gift money on lessons—piano and voice—given me by a choirmaster in the town where I was at school. I used to practise at his house. It was more fun to me than larking around with my schoolmates. When I was about seventeen, my mother became very ill and knew that she could not recover. But before she died she told me the whole history of her marriage and why she had left America. She said she felt at last that it had all been a mistake and begged me to try and find my father, who seemed to have disappeared from public life in some mysterious way. She could give me no clue to him except the address of his former lawyers in New York. I in my turn confessed to her that I had been studying voice and piano music and hoped sometime to devote my life to it. She forgave me my deception, acknowledging that the music was in my blood and that she saw it would be useless to fight it any longer.

"After she died, I finished my schooling and took two years of music in Paris. Then I came to America. That was about five or six years ago. I had got in touch with my father's former lawyers at once after my mother's death, but they could tell me nothing about him except that he had completely disappeared. I've been searching for him, off and on, ever since.

"When I first got to this country I had very little money left, so I naturally turned to my music to earn it. I tried giving concerts and recitals in various parts of America, but found it hard to get a foothold. At last I became connected with a big radio-broadcasting company and met with quite a little success.

"It was not pure chance that I happened to take my vacation here. I've always been fond of fishing, and had heard someone tell of this wild stretch of beach and also of a strange man called the 'Hermit' who lived here and owned a famous 'Strad.' So I decided to try it. I hadn't the faintest idea that it was going to bring me so near to the father I'd been searching for so long. But I hoped the violin might prove interesting. That very first morning, as I got near his shack, I saw him outside chopping wood and decided to go over and have a chat with him. But he caught sight of me first, and to my amazement darted inside and slammed his door. After that I didn't quite like to go and disturb him. Then I saw the children coming along and was still more surprised when they told me they were bound for that very shack on an errand. I thought he must be a crank of some kind.

"Then, you remember, I asked you about him that evening, Mr. Danby, and you gave me quite a description of him. Something about it particularly caught my attention—perhaps it was a suggestion of mystery —and I decided to keep an eye on him. You never got a chance to tell me about the violin. I think you were going to, that night, when little Miss Marcella here had the accident with the ink bottle. After that I guess the subject was forgotten."

"Oh," burst out Marcella, to the surprise of everyone, "I *wish* I hadn't done it! It was on purpose, because I was listening, and I knew Daddy was going to speak of that, and I thought—er—Mr. Seymour had acted as if he didn't want you to know about that— or anything about him. So I thought of doing that as the only way to stop Daddy. I'm so sorry!" Big tears gathered in her eyes, but the Hermit soothed her chagrin by saying:

"That wasn't your fault at all, my dear, it was mine —it was just a mistake all around. I'm proud really of the way you tried to show your loyalty!" And that unexpected praise pleased Marcella beyond words.

"Well, there isn't a great deal more to tell," went on Mr. Robinson. "During the days of the storm, I frequently walked down as far as the shack, but never happened to catch sight of my father. On the last day, however, I tramped down on the Bay side, for the sake of shelter as much as anything, and when I got to the path that led across the dunes to his shack, I noticed a motorboat moored near it. It was no boat I had remembered seeing, and something about it struck me as a little queer—even sinister. Perhaps it was seeing it there in that bad storm. So I decided to hide myself in the bushes and find out what it was all about. I hadn't been there long, when I saw the figure of this Mr. Seymour limping along pulling a sand-sled behind him. I supposed he was going to get some wood from the big pile there. I had almost decided to appear and offer to help him when I saw him stop short, evidently at the sight of the boat, stare at it almost in horror, and then turn and hurry back to the ocean side.

"The whole thing made me very curious, but I

didn't like to follow right after him, so I stayed where I was for a while. Then the strangest thing of all happened. For down the path hot-foot there a young man came dashing. He was breathless and hatless, and his clothes looked as if he had been through a fight or struggle of some kind. But, stranger than that, he was carrying a violin in one hand. It took me only a second to realize that it was an old and rare one. Then I took another look at his face, and realized, with a shock of astonishment, that it was the same fellow I had met on a steamer coming back from Europe this fall. He had been swaggering about, talking of how he had been sent here to look up rare violins by an Italian nobleman who wanted a few to add to his collection. And in an unguarded moment, which I later greatly regretted, I mentioned to him what I had heard about a strange, hermit-like man living down on the coast who possessed what he claimed was a genuine Strad. Of course, I had never known about the trouble my father had had with someone claiming it, or I should never have mentioned the thing. The young man's reputation on the boat had been none too good, and even then I suspected him of fraud of some kind.

"And then I stumbled across him, racing down to

his boat as if pursued, and clutching a rare violin in his hand. That was too much! It was perfectly plain to me that he must have stolen it and had had *some* fight before he got it. So without giving him a chance to think, I just stepped out of my hiding-place and faced him. All I said was, 'Hand over that violin—and be quick about it!'

"He was so stunned that I believe he was just about to do it, too! But he must have suddenly thought better of it. For without a word, and like a streak of lightning, he ducked sideways into the bushes and got the start of me by a number of yards before I got my wits together to chase him up. And it was *some* chase he led me too, before it was over! But I guess he wasn't much used to running. Back nearly to where we started from, I caught up with him and grabbed the violin out of his hands. It's a wonder it wasn't wrecked during that chase!

"He blubbered and blustered and whined about its having been stolen from his family years before and he'd just found out where it was. I gave him just five minutes to get in his boat and beat it for parts unknown. I told him he could consider himself lucky that I wasn't reporting him to the police. He hadn't much fight left in him and was pretty well exhausted and I think my remark about the police rather disturbed him. Anyway, he crawled aboard and five minutes later had chugged away out of sight. Then I returned to the shack to restore the lost violin, from which I surmised it had been taken. I first wrapped it in an old steamer blanket that he'd left lying on the shore. I could see in the hasty glance I gave it that it was a Strad and a beauty. And it somehow made me think of my father.

"When I got back to the hut, I glanced in and saw you all in there. Then I knocked—and you know what happened after that. It was my father's unconscious cry about 'Solange' and 'the boy' that suddenly made me realize what the possibility might be. It was not till he asked me who I was that I decided to try an experiment. And instead of answering him, I took the violin and played the little cradle song that he had composed for me. My mother before she died had told me its history, and so I knew where it had originated and that no one except my father himself would ever recognize it. And you were there to see the effect it had. And that's all the story, I think, except to say that this is the happiest thing that has ever happened to me!"

There was a long sigh of relaxed tension from

everyone when he came to the end. Then it was Jack who suddenly piped up:

"Wasn't it lucky that Mr. Robinson had heard about your Strad? But I wonder how that Tony Giotto discovered where you lived?"

"That we'll probably never know," admitted the Hermit, "but it may have been that after his request in the paper for information about violins, someone who has at some time been here and happened to see my instrument had informed him of its whereabouts. I have had stray visitors at times, people who drifted in here in strolling down the beach or who came in to see the museum. And I have never made a secret of the violin if they showed any interest in it.

It was Mr. Danby who made the next inquiry. "May I ask," he said, "if you two have made any plans? I hope we are not going to lose you here. The beach would be lonely without you. And yet I'm sure you will want to be near your son."

"We have talked of that," admitted the Hermit, "and have both arrived at one conclusion. And that is, to go on very much as we have been doing. I am too old to change my mode of life now. It suits me perfectly, and I have no desire to return to public life. I shall even remain 'Herbert Seymour' and avoid all undue publicity. And my son has his way to make and is well started in his music. It will be foolish for him to change his life also. But we shall be together as often as possible here, and are content that we have found each other."

"And what about the violin?" timidly questioned Marcella.

"I have given it to my son," declared the Hermit, "in exchange for a very good though not famous one that he himself owns. Then I can make music here when I please, and give Miss Marcella the violin lessons I hear she is so anxious to take. And as for you, Jack and Jill, I suggest that you come down to the museum some day, and let me give you two rare old bottles for your collection. It is the least I can do, after all you children did for me!"

"Oh, *boy!*" chorused Jack and Jill, and after that, there seemed nothing more to say. The story had all been told, the mystery was solved at last, and the Hermit was looking a bit weary after the excitement of the telling of it. His son noticed the look and rose.

"You'd better be getting to bed, Father. You aren't entirely fit just yet, you know. But before we go up, would you care to play that little cradle song of mine on the Strad, and I'll accompany you on the piano?"

"Gladly!" said the Hermit, and took his violin from where it had rested on his knee, tuned it a bit, and tucked it under his chin. His son sat down at the piano, played a few chords, and then they both slipped into the enchanting little tune. The other four listened spellbound to the hushed melody. And when it had died away, the two players said a quiet good-night and went away upstairs, leaving the others still sitting about the fireplace.

No one spoke for quite a while. There didn't seem to be any words into which they could put their thoughts. But presently Mr. Danby spoke:

"The thing that seems as marvelous as any to me is the way you children helped to rescue the Hermit from the marsh that first day. What a catastrophe it would have been if you hadn't happened along there!"

Suddenly Jill came to life and began counting on her fingers, much to their amazement. "That's the word!" she cried. "The one I've been hunting for three days—*catastrophe*—eleven letters, means 'a very disastrous happening'—and fits right into my cross-word puzzle! You needn't laugh!" she added, as the rest broke into a gale of merriment at her sudden inspiration. "Now that the mystery's solved, I suppose we'll have to get back to crossword puzzles to take up our spare time!"

A little later, when Mrs. Burdick had called her children to go up to bed, Marcella still remained, snuggled down by her father on the couch before the fire. Presently she burrowed her head in his shoulder and sighed happily:

"Oh, Daddy—wasn't it *too wonderful!*"